MICHAEL CONLEY

BELLA

Wild West Press

Louisville, KY

𝔚𝔦𝔩𝔡 𝔚𝔢𝔰𝔱 𝔓𝔯𝔢𝔰𝔰

Thank you for reading! If you like the book, please leave a review on Amazon and Goodreads. Even if you don't like it, please still leave a review.

MICHAEL CONLEY

BELLA

CHAPTER ONE – WASCO

"Red Legs are attacking! Red Legs are attacking!"

"Shut up, they are not, it's only one person," I elbowed Josh in his ribs. "What kind of attack would one Native be, chucklehead?"

"You don't know everything, Topher! What if it's a shaman come to make another curse?" Josh said.

"Yer a chucklehead. You ain't even ever seen no shaman! Nobody has and there ain't been no curses in a hundred years! Wait here, I'll get my pa's ol' spyglass and show ya."

I climbed down from the balcony of the old boarded up hotel and took off through the muddy streets. The buildings of the city proper loomed high above, reaching for the cloudless sky. A glint from one of the glass windows caught my eye and I wondered if the people up there were watching me as I ran through the narrow streets of the Ends.

As I passed an apple cart, I reached behind a customer, grabbed an apple, and kept running. No calls followed me, so I smiled and took a bite as I sprinted toward home. I turned down my street, which was really an ally any respectable street would be offended to have been compared with, and skipped through the legs of some mutated Foggies.

I still didn't know why the steam from the Ember mines made some people sick and not others, but the people we called Foggies had gotten the worst of it. They were the unfortunates that clung to life, even if it meant begging for scraps and living in misery. The mutations weren't all bad though. I remember a man who lived a few rows over that had made good use of his. He could compress his body, much like a rat and squeeze into places others couldn't. He did some work in the mines, but I think now he might have been using his skills for thievery. He lived in the Ends with the rest the poor people, but never seemed to be without food or good clothes. Most who were inflicted chose the Edge, the cliff that gave the city its name and broke the continent in half. They would throw themselves off to fall past the mines which were the cause of their pain and crash to the Blacklands below. That day though, they were just another obstacle in the streets for my young feet to dance past without a second thought.

Our house was a one-room shack in a row of one-room shacks. I think they had been tool sheds back when the mines first opened, but they were better than the streets. Most of my friends didn't have any house at all, so I was lucky. I ducked through the curtain that was our front door and ripped the old canvas bag out from under the bed and found the worn leather case that held the spyglass. Without bothering to replace the bag, I tore back out the door and down the street. Ma wouldn't be home till the end of the week, so I would just put it back later. I danced back past the Foggies and weaved in and out of people going about their daily chores. Little swirls of fog followed in my wake.

When I got back I shimmied up the post and shoved William and Josh to either side to get the best view of the supposed Red Legs.

Bella

William's pa was a miner and his ma stayed home but hadn't paid him much mind. He liked to pretend he was the leader of our little group. His father beat him bad sometimes, so I guess he needed to be in control of something in his life. Some kids who got beat like him took to bullying, others took to getting bullied, but William didn't do either. He was a good friend and funny enough to not have to fight other kids.

Josh and Sandy were orphans. Josh split his loyalties between me and William and Sandy was just quiet and went where the wind blew. I don't know what Sandy's real name was; I just know it wasn't Sandy. Everyone just called him that because of his light brown hair and eyes.

I was somewhere between orphan and not. My ma worked the mines and my pa was gone years now, so I was mostly alone and running the streets, but at least I had a house to go to on cold nights. I guess independence caused me to be more assertive than some. Not that we were a gang or had a real leader or anything. It was just one of those things that kids did, one always taking the lead.

I looked out and found the figure across the snow-blown plane and locked my eyes on it while I pulled out the spyglass. They were a lot closer now and they definitely looked like they were wearing red leggings like a Native. Not that *all* Natives wore red leggings, just one tribe did, but they were the most aggressive tribe in the area, and the only one people were truly afraid of even though they hadn't done anything to warrant fear in years. Unlike most tribes, they didn't stay in the Nations and were said to still attack people traveling to and from the city.

The spyglass made a *clunk, clunk, clunk* as I opened it to its full length and raised it to my eye. I couldn't see anything at first, just an array of colors streaking around the lens. I was trying to hurry so I could show off how cool the spyglass was before the figure got so close everyone could see it anyway, but all I got for my efforts were blurs of motion. I remembered when I was little my pa telling Ma she had to move the spyglass slow when he was showing her how to use it. I looked up from it and marked the spot again, then slowly raised the glass back to my eye and moved it very slowly. I caught a flash of bright red-fringed leggings and I sucked in a breath. Maybe it was a Red Legs!

"What is it Topher?" William asked.

"I'm still looking, shut up chucklehead," I said.

William tried to snatch the spyglass, causing me to lose sight of the figure again. After winning a tussle for control I found the red pants again and slowly raised the glass up past the fur cloak to the face buried beneath a thick dark beard streaked with grey. The wind blew his beard to the side and I noticed a bone choker around his neck, like those the natives favored.

His face was weathered and old and had the dark look of the Native tribes, but this was no Red Legs, he was just an old mountain man.

"He ain't no Red Legs," I said.

I handed over the spyglass to William.

"Aw, he's just an old trapper." William's voice reeked of disappointment after a minute of looking. "I seen his type before at the General when I was sweepin'." He stood up and tossed the spyglass at me.

I yelled at him, "Be careful, that was my pa's from the war!"

"Lemme see," Sandy whined.

"Don't bother Sandy," William told him, "It's just an old trapper. Let's go cut some drinker root, mine's wore out. Coming Topher?"

I looked back at the man in the red leggings. He was walking right down the old wagon road that was used when the city was just a little mining town called The End of the World. Then they built Edge City and the old town became the slums that they called The Ends. I guessed he didn't know he couldn't get through that way.

"Na, my spitshot's still good, I'm gonna see if I can get a penny or two from that there guy," I said. "Looks like he's lost."

The others climbed down after William.

"See ya later, mud face," William called up once he was on the street and took off running as he laughed. The others echoed him with calls of, "See ya, mud-face!" as they ran.

I chucked the apple core I had been chewing on at William but missed.

"Stupid chuckleheaded ghost!" I shouted after him.

He always liked to make fun of my brown skin. I loved my brown skin and mass of curly hair. Everyone else I knew was white, so I figured it made me special.

"Gonna shove *his* face in some mud one of these days," I mumbled and stuck the spyglass into the waist of my britches.

I climbed back down the pole and headed to the section of wall the stranger was headed toward. I ignored the dirty looks of a couple of Enlightened followers preaching the perils of the city for not worshiping the Enlightened Emperor. I knew they thought themselves my better because they were white skinned. Luckily, there weren't many Enlightened who lived here, so they didn't take it any further than preaching and giving me a glare. I showed them my middle finger. In some parts they would gang up on what they called lesser races and beat them. In the Ends they knew better.

I followed Main Street until it dead-ended at the wooden wall surrounding the city and then peeked through the slats to find the mountain man standing there staring at the fence like it was going to open for him.

"Closest gates about a two-mile walk," I called between the slats of the wall, sticking my face through.

The city was completely walled in except where it hit the mountain or the cliff that gave it its name. Down in the Ends where I lived, the wall was more of a fence. It was left over from when the Ends was just a small mining town and was barely maintained at all, even though it was the part of the city closest to the Red Legs Tribes.

His eyes flicked over to where I had stuck my face through and his forehead creased a little. He looked left and right, then back at the wall the old road dead-ended into. He didn't move for what seemed like minutes, like he was a stone that had rolled out of the mountains and just happened to stop there.

I said, "I know how you can get in if you don't wanna go around. If you gimme a penny, I'll show ya."

With a slight nod of his chin, he said, "Fine".

The word rolled out of him, tentative but deep and gravelly. Almost like his voice had been uncovered in a rockslide.

I had him shadow me to an old fence post about a block down behind an old warehouse. The wall was nothing but wooden pickets and most of it was old and rarely repaired. When they did fix it, it was with a few cheap nails in the same old holes, which made them loose and the wood soft. All the kids knew about it. I climbed onto the post and hung from it, pulling hard. It shifted with my pull and made a slight screech as the nails pulled out of the rails.

The fence sagged, and the bottom hit hard in the dirt before leaning forward, pulling mostly free on the far end with a sharp squeal. The result was a man-sized opening even the trapper could fit through. Once he did I pulled the fence back against the leaning post. Someone would come by later and put new nails in without securing the post in the ground but I would still be able to open it.

He was a big man, but not as big as I remember thinking he was at first. He was hairy and rough with crystal blue eyes that made me shiver. Sure enough he was wearing Red Leg leggings and moccasins, a linen shirt covered with a fringed buckskin jacket and furs that smelled wet. He would be an intimidating man to most, I imagined. His hair was streaked with grey and as unkempt as his white streaked beard.

I held out my hand, "Gimme a penny or I'm gonna yell for the guards and tell them you broke the fence"

He looked down at me, "What's yer name?"

"I'm Christopher, but everyone calls me Topher."

"You sound like a girl," he said.

"I am a girl, lushington! Maybe you ought a lay off the bottle!" I said. "I got a boy's name like the girls in the Capital do! They all get boys names ya know. Pa wanted me to be a lady like them."

He made a noise that sounded like two stones being rubbed together.

"Ok, Topher," he said. "My name's Wasco and I ain't got no money. But if you take me somewhere I can trade these pelts, I'll give ya three pennies when I sell 'em. If I can buy a rifle there too, I'll give you a nickel."

"Sonofabitch. You said you had a penny!" I yelled.

"No, I said fine, you assumed that meant I had a penny," he said.

"Better not be lying this time," I said, and pushed past him to stalk up the street.

He caught up to me and said, "You an African, are ya?"

"No, I fell face-first into a mud hole!" I said looking at him sidewise. "Of course I'm African. Pa used to say we wasn't, said Africans weren't as good as others so we was supposed to say we was from somewhere else. I forget where. He fought for the Enlightenment in the war. Ma said he was a no-good cocksucker though, and that we ain't no less than anyone and we're African."

"How come you don't live in the Nation? Most Africans live in the Nation these days."

"'Cause we live here. Never been to the Nation."

He didn't say anything else, just kept walking and looking around. At times he seemed to know which way to go, but he would stop sometimes and wait for me to show him and make that rumbling grunt. I led him to the General because it was the closest store I could think of that sold furs and guns and wouldn't throw us out.

Wasco walked in and began talking to the clerk. I pocketed a few pieces of hard candy while they were busy before walking over to listen.

"What the hell is this?" I heard Wasco say.

He was holding a steam rifle and looking at it like the man had just handed him cow dung.

"Why that's the Sam Thomson Steam Powered T-17. Best rifle on the market. You want a rifle worthy of the name, that's the one!" the clerk said.

He wasn't the owner. I knew the owner because he would never take his eyes off me long enough for me to take the candy which was filling my pockets. This guy must have been new. He was kind of young and very enthusiastic about selling things.

"This ain't no goddamned rifle, son. I ain't sure what this is, but it ain't no damned rifle," Wasco growled.

"I assure you it is the top of the line, good sir. One gram of Ember will fuel it for a month, you just refill the reservoir." His clean fingernail tapped the screw cap on the stock. "Of course, you'll need bullets as well," the clerk said with a fake chuckle, then reached under the counter and produced a box of ammo. Wasco eyed the box then looked back at the clerk.

"Got somethin' that uses gun powder?" he asked.

"Oh, you're looking for an antique! I thought…well, you seemed like a man that knows how to use a rifle is all. No sir, we don't carry anything like that, only the newest and the best at the General!" the clerk said.

"And how much is this newest and best?" Wasco asked.

"That's only ninety-five dollars my friend, and I'll toss in the Ember and the ammo for just five dollars more!" the clerk responded.

"Yer kidding me. This mess a tubes and copper costs near a hundred dollars? Ya only gave me twenty-nine fer those pelts!"

The clerk was starting back into his sales pitch when the door jingled, creaked, slammed, and three uniformed men walked in.

"I'll be a son of a whore; we got a real live Red Legs right here in the store? I thought you ran a clean place here, Ned," one of them said loudly.

Wasco handed the steam rifle back to the clerk.

"I'll just take the money for the pelts."

The newcomers came up to the counter and gathered around Wasco, who didn't spare them a glance. The loudmouth leaned around to look at Wasco and saw his white face and beard and stepped back.

"Sorry 'bout that mister. You runnin' around in them red pants, well you looked like one of those horse-sucking savages. You take them from a dead one? You ain't one of them Native-loving types that do men's business with savages are ya?" He said the last with a fist bump to one of the others' arm and they laughed.

Wasco turned his head as slow as a growing mountain and looked at him. His eyes slid down to the little badge the man wore on his collar, it had two letters in a set of wings. K.I. They were Keaton's men, steamship flyers home from a trip. Wasco's hand reached out, still slow as could be, grabbed the little badge between thick fingers and pulled. There was a ripping sound as the badge came loose.

"What's this?" He turned the badge towards the man's face.

"What in the hell? It's my damn badge and you got you an ass whoopin' comin' for tearin' my blues!"

He hauled his fist back and took a swing that looked like it came all the way from the Capital. Even I could have gotten out the way. My ma could've. Wasco didn't move. His head snapped to the right a little when the fist hit him, then slowly turned back to the man, eyes going hard.

"I said, what is this?" He held the badge up again. "What is K.I.?"

I spoke up. "It's Keaton Industries; Keaton pretty much owns Edge City."

The man was just staring at Wasco and flexing his hand.

Wasco's voice grated across the air again. "You fly in one of those ships? The ones that fly with bags of air or somethin'?"

Still unsure what to make of the situation, the man nodded his head.

"When?" Wasco asked.

"When what?"

"When did you last fly in one of them ships?" Wasco repeated.

"What the hell does it matter? You tore my damn uniform, now we're gonna tear your ass! Grab him Bob!"

One of his buddies had walked behind Wasco and tried to grab him in a bear hug. He might as well have tried to grab an actual bear. Loudmouth let fly with another punch and this time Wasco did move. Without any apparent effort he broke the hug and caught the punch on his thick forearm as his other fist slammed into Loudmouth's ribs.

11

I heard an awful crunch and Loudmouth fell to the floor wheezing. The man behind Wasco wrapped his arms around him again, trying to lift him. Wasco started moving backwards, gaining speed, and they crashed into the wall, knocking a cow skull to the floor. I heard the air leave the man's body in a whoosh. Wasco's head snapped back and Bob's nose exploded.

When Wasco stepped forward, Bob crumpled to the ground gasping for air and choking on blood. The last guy came running towards Wasco screaming. The clerk was yelling for help, everything was going crazy! I was hiding behind a shelf shoving candy into pockets that couldn't hold any more.

Loudmouth got back to his feet reaching for his gun.
"Wasco, gun!"

I don't know why I yelled. It wasn't my fight. I think I just wanted to be sure those assholes didn't steal the money he owed me.

Wasco's huge fist met the runner's face and stood him up straight. He stayed there for a second before falling backwards stiff as a board. Loudmouth's gun came up and went off. I couldn't tell if it hit Wasco or not. I was sure it could not have missed, but Wasco just reached down to his belt, pulled out a Native's tomahawk and threw it in one smooth motion. It sang out a "*ka-thunk*" as it stuck through Loudmouth's boot, foot, and into the wooden floor. He shrieked and dropped his gun. Dumbass. He tried to reach for the axe. Wasco took two long steps and his long knife met the man's nose before he could bend over far enough to retrieve his weapon, stopping him in mid-move. Wasco then stood him back up by slowly raising the knife.

"How long has it been since you last flew that ship? When did you get back? Did you rustle any horses?" Wasco growled.

A trickle of blood ran from Loudmouth's nose and trailed along his lip before forming a small drop on his chin. Bob made a pained groan behind Wasco and fell as he tried to stand.

"UhummmIdunno!" Loudmouth said. "Maybe a couple a months? We don't fly all the time; we do some time on the ground and some time on the ships, I dunno! Horses? Why in the hell would we rustle horses? The boss would kill us!"

Wasco stared at him for a few seconds that passed like a cold winter night, sheathed his knife, bent, and pulled the hawk from the guy's foot. He turned and grabbed the coin from the counter for his pelts and without a look to the befuddled clerk, walked out the door. I followed him out as Loudmouth hit the floor passed out cold. Pansy *and* a dumbass.

We stopped on the porch and Wasco took a stubby cigar from a pocket and struck a match with his thumb. Once it lit he looked down at me.

"Where the hell can I buy a *real* gun in this town?" he asked.

Blood ran down his hand from a hole in his bicep. He *had* been shot and hadn't even flinched. Didn't even seem to notice. I watched the blood as it ran down his forearm and hand. I'd never seen someone get shot before. It was almost hypnotic watching the blood run from the hole to his fingertip. I could swear I saw it swirling in little patterns around the wound.

"You been shot."

He looked at the arm. "Yeah," he said.
"You need a doctor?"
"No, I need a rifle."
I shrugged. "Old Ying probably has one. Come on."

CHAPTER TWO – YING

I still wasn't sure if Wasco had ever been to the city. He walked confidently, as if he had lived there his whole life, but he damn sure didn't know his way around and he looked at everyday things like he'd never seen their like before. I took him the long way around since he seemed interested in things and I figured if he thought it took longer I could get another penny from him. When we passed Heaven's Gate he stopped and looked up the road.

"What's that?" he asked with a nod of his head.

"What, the carriage? It's a steam carriage. Where the hell you been?" I answered.

"Was askin' 'bout through them gates. Don't remember this being here. Come to think of it, the carriage too. Where the hell are the horses?"

"Ain't no horses, it works on steam and Ember," I said.

"Ember?" he asked.

I looked over to see if he was serious.

"Losin' all that blood got you dragged out? Ember! You know, steam rock? Black rock? Come on, where you been?"

"Ain't never heard of it. How's that make a carriage go without a horse?" He kept talking like he's been stuck in a cave.

"It's the same as that gun you were gawkin' at in the General. When you put Ember in water it makes steam, and the steam makes things go. Everybody knows that! That's why Mr. Keaton's so rich; he found a whole slew of the stuff right under the city. Back before I was even born," I said.

"That what's causing all that steam?"

"I guess. But most people here in the Ends can't afford to use it much. Steam mostly comes up over the cliff and through cracks in the ground from the mines. They use water to wash out the mines, and when it goes over the side it makes steam," I said.

It was like talking to a baby. I couldn't understand how someone could not know about Ember.

"The Ends?" he asked. "Is that what you call the town now?"

"Naw, the Ends is just this part of the city. Where the poor folk live. Over there is the market, and over there the factory district. We're going to the Chinese Quarter by the factories. And that up there is Heaven, that's where the rich people live. I hear there ain't no steam in the streets up there so when they look down, the steam clouds down here makes it look like they're in Heaven," I said, pointing through the gate.

"Never been?" he asked.

"Naw, they don't let Ends folks up there less they got work to do, and that ain't many," I said. "Most folk work in the mines; if they got any work at all."

He started walking again, limping a bit, and glancing back at the gates or the steam carriage, I'm not sure which.

"You hurt?" I asked.

"Old," he said. "Damn knee locks up sometimes is all. It'll work itself out."

The Chinese Quarter was the worst part of the city. It was a mixture of run-down abandoned warehouses, and homemade buildings of cloth, wood, and waxed paper. A few places, like Ying's, had glass doors, but very few. Steam was so thick most days you couldn't see ten feet ahead. Many of the people here wore clothes tied over their faces or masks, but it didn't help. It was still full of Foggies.

"Why is there so much more steam here?" he asked.

"I dunno. They're the only ones that get it worse than us. We get it when the wind shifts, but it blows out sooner or later. Here steam just sits all the time. No wind 'cause of the hill. That's why they get more Foggies than anybody else."

He looked at me oddly at the word, but in short order it was clear what I was talking about. The lame and mutated were all around. We had our share in my neighborhood, but here they were all over. Faces or arms wrapped in cotton, some with arms or legs too big or too small, heads covered and deformed. It made me sad to see them. Even now thinking of them makes my heart break.

"What's with them?" he nodded toward a group of young men standing in an alley, staring at us.

"Nothin', just walk on by. Don't worry, they know me," I said.

"I wasn't worried 'bout 'em girl, just wonderin' why they were given *me* the stink eye, and what's with the scar on their necks?"

"I don't know. Ying says a lot of the young men have them these days and said they was trouble and to stay away from 'em. I think they won't bother us 'cause I know her, but ain't no sense tempting 'em so come on!" I said.

He followed, staring them down for a long while. They didn't look away. I would have. He had a stare that made your blood run cold, but they held his stare until we turned.

We came 'round the corner and could see Ying's store at the end of the road. I had known Ying since I was old enough to run the streets. She looked out for me and I ran errands for her. Not a lot of round-eyes were allowed as much freedom as I was here. Customers of her shop were lucky if they got out of the Quarter with everything they came in with. But they did still come. Mostly young men wanting powdered rhino horn and to visit the laundries, laundries being the whore houses in the Chinese quarter.

The shop was at the end of a street where the only breeze in the Quarter somehow kept the steam away. One step you were wet with it, the next you were in a cool dry semicircle facing the glass door and window of the shop. Big gold letters surrounding two entwined dragons and some Chinese symbols read *Ying's Shop of Celestial Wonders*.

We walked up, and Wasco opened the door to the sound of wooden tubes that tinkled and tonged melodically. Old Ying called it bamboo. She had a garden where it grew behind the shop and little plants of it inside. The sound made me feel safe and at ease. Even Wasco looked more relaxed as he went in.

"Can I help you? You look for powdered horn of rhino to entertain your girl?"

"What?" Wasco said.

I stepped around Wasco and glared at the young Chinese man dressed in overly ornate traditional garb to impress the customers. His name was Li. He was Old Ying's manservant.

"Ain't like you never seen me afore dumbass! You sayin' I'm a whore now? And why you talkin' like that?"

"Oh! I didn't see you at first young Topher. I am sorry!" Li, looking chagrined, replied without the exaggerated accent he used for the dumb customers.

He bent at the waist toward me and then to Wasco and said, "What can I help you find? We have many wonders from faraway lands."

"I need a rifle"," Wasco growled. "A real one, not one of them steam-powered ditties. Lemme see that one."

He gestured at a rifle that sat on a top shelf. It looked like it was a hundred years old, with a dragon carved into its barrel. I'm not sure I had ever seen it before, but there were so many things in Ying's shop it was hard to say.

"Oh, I am afraid that is not for sale," Li said.

"Why the hell would it be in a store with a tag hangin' from it if it wasn't for sale?" Wasco asked.

"Oh, ah, well, many things you know..."

He was still stuttering when Old Ying stepped out from behind the curtain in the back of the store.

"Ah, Christopher, you brought me a customer. How are you? How is your mother?"

She always called me by my full name.

"Ma's ok, down in the mines doin' a shift."

Old Ying's face drooped a little at that, for a moment showing the weight of her years. She looked up at Wasco.

"Mr. Wasco, welcome to my shop. I see you have a keen eye for weapons. I think that would serve as a suitable substitute."

She pointed at the rifle with her walking stick. "Fetch me the rifle, Li. I will show you how fine a rifle that is Mr.

Wasco, but first, let me see that arm before you get blood on everything in my shop."

Wasco gave her a puzzled look and looked down at his arm as if he had forgotten. He then took off his fur cloak and fringed deerskin jacket. The shirt and arm both had a hole in it and were leaking blood, but not nearly as much as they had been. The sleeve had turned completely red. He looked down at it and frowned a bit. Ying tore the shirt sleeve and began dabbing the wound with a cloth she produced from her pocket.

"Li, get me some water. It looks to have passed through without much damage, Mr. Wasco," she said.

"Ya, I know."

She gave him a momentary scowl. She cleaned the wound with the cloth and water Li brought, covered it in a sweet-smelling paste and wrapped it in clean linen. Li, meanwhile, had found a stool and brought down the rifle for her. When she finished he held it out to Ying, but she shifted her eyes to Wasco, so he held it out to him. Wasco took it, looking from him to her and then at the rifle. It was a fine piece of craftsmanship. I didn't think it would shoot a dang thing, but it was pretty.

"Does it shoot?" Wasco asked.

"Oh yes," Ying answered.

"How much? I can't read this."

He held up a little white tag with a symbol on it.

"Oh, never mind that," she said, "I will sell it to you for fifty-two dollars. That is very cheap for such an item."

Li's eyes widened and he looked as if he was going to say something but kept quiet, apparently with some effort.

"What the hell makes it worth fifty-two damn dollars? It shoot gold?" Wasco asked.

She smiled a small wrinkled smile and shook her head. "No Mr. Wasco, not gold. It shoots fire."

"Huh?" Wasco said.

"This is a Chinese fire rifle, Mr. Wasco. Crafted in my home country. It will shoot regular lead balls just as any western rifle does but will also shoot these." She motioned with her tiny hand towards a small box of odd-colored metal balls.

Wasco looked unimpressed.

"I see, you think this old woman is trying to play games on a round-eye to cheat him of his hard-earned coin. No, Mr. Wasco, let me demonstrate."

With that she grabbed one of the metal balls and walked through the cluttered aisles, walking stick thumping rhythmically on the wooden floorboards.

"Come along," she said over her shoulder.

She didn't wait to see if anyone followed, just walked through a curtain into the back of the store and out an old rickety door that we heard slam. By the time we reached her she was standing in the alley waiting for us. She handed Wasco the odd-looking metal ball and nodded down the alley.

"Go ahead, just like you always have, and do aim for the brick wall, not the wood"," she instructed.

With the surety of years of experience Wasco popped a load of powder down the barrel, tapped it, hesitated a moment looking at Old Ying, and finally took the ball and shoved it down the barrel.

He set a cap into place, took aim at a spot on a brick wall down the alley and squeezed the trigger. The cap fired, and smoke shot from the barrel with a roar. When the ball hit the wall, it burst into a ball of flame as big as a man's head and caught a nearby crate on fire. Li ran down to stomp it out, catching his britches aflame. The next few minutes were some of the funniest in my life.

Once we had the fire out, Li's bum covered, and some salve on the small burns he had gotten for his trouble, Old Ying looked at Wasco.

"So, Old Ying did not lie to you," she said.

She patted his hand. Wasco, still holding the rifle, looked at it and back to her.

"It is a fine rifle. It'll shoot regular lead too?" he asked.

She nodded.

"I ain't got that kinda money," he said. "That's the truth of it, so no sense going into any sales shake. I just ain't got it. I did see as you've got a Cooper double-action in the case. How much for that?"

"Oh, that old thing? You can have it for ten dollars."

Wasco's eyebrows made a V and his eyes narrowed, and she smiled.

"Five dollars then and done. As to the rifle, I think we may be able to work something out. Are you willing to do some work for the difference?" she asked.

"I could do that. What did you have in mind?" he asked.

"Just a couple of small errands is all. First, there is a girl in the Quarter that runs a bath and barber. I think she may be in some danger from some of Heaven's young men that like to come make trouble. I do not know what she did to offend them, but I am hearing they have taken to coming in once a week and running off all her customers. I hesitate to ask you to put yourself in danger, but perhaps if you were there when they arrived they would think twice"."

"They carry iron?"

"No, not that I am aware of. But just in case, Li get the pistol from the case for Mr. Wasco. You can pay when you return. I will discount the rifle twenty-two dollars making it an even thirty dollars if you'll do this."

"Still ain't got enough I'm afraid," Wasco said.

"Then I will find other things for you to do, Mr. Wasco." She smiled that smile that made wrinkles appear all over her tiny face. "Now, as chance would have it, those young men are due this very day. If you rush over now, you should beat them there."

Wasco grunted, nodded, and stood up. I did too.

"No, I need you here Christopher, and that side of town is no place for a young lady.

I was going to argue, but I never won with Old Ying, so I let him go and vowed to find out everything later.

A couple hours later the chimes on the door sang their song and Wasco walked in, or more accurately, a Wasco-like being walked in. His beard was trimmed close to his face, with the stray whiskers having been cut into clean lines. His hair had been cropped short above his ears and collar and exposed his bright blue eyes.

He might have been called handsome now, the dark hair complimenting blue eyes, but when the blue eyes flicked around the room taking in every detail, it felt more like the gaze of a predator and I wished the long greasy bangs were still there to hide them.

He pulled out his short cigar and walked over to lean against the wall. A look to Old Ying who frowned kept him from lighting it.

"Well, I headed down the way you told me," he started without preamble. "The steam is pretty thick down that way. Most folk wear masks I notice. I stopped into the saloon I passed thinkin' to grab a drink, but they ain't even have whiskey. Gave me something called sake instead. Ain't gonna stay in business serving that swill.

"Couple of them boys with the scars on their necks were following me and was waiting outside of the saloon when I came back out. Weren't even tryin' to stay out of sight."

At this Ying nodded as if that meant something but didn't say anything.

"I turned there at the washhouse you told me 'bout. Them the girls you say are whorin'? Seems so. Made me wonder if the bath and barber was gonna be a whorehouse too.

"When I got there the boys on my tail settled in across the street same as they had before. I went in and this little slip of a girl asked if she could help me. She was lookin' nervous soon as I come in. I could tell she'd rather I not be there. I stayed anyway and sat down for the first hair cutting I had since I walked into the mountains."

He scowled. "Suppose it was long overdue. I was tryin' to stall so I had her start with just a little but had to have her keep going and get into my beard too. Ain't been this short in a long time. She kept tryin' to hurry me out.

"Thought I was gonna have to have her shave me clean until a couple of young dandies swaggered in. They eyed me right away and kept up staring like they meant to run me off. I didn't pay 'em no mind and kept getting this and that trimmed. I did notice Win's hands started shaking a bit. That was her name by the way. Win.

"Their next play was to surround me and tell me I ought to leave. I opted for a bath instead, can't say that made 'em happy. Thought for a minute the big one might step up, but he simmered down once I was lookin' down on him. Wasn't as big as he thought he was when I was standin'." He stopped, and a slick smile crossed his face.

"I set a quarter on the counter and walked to the back of the place and behind the curtain and called out for some hot water. I made a show of dropping my gun belt and britches. Well, I made it sound like I did anyway, then I waited. I figured if they was gonna make a go of it that would have been the time. They didn't, so I inched up to the curtain and peeked out. That's when I knew what was going on. Four of them was talking about who was gonna come throw me out. The leader of their bunch was leaning in close, talking to Win. But gentle like.

"He had her hand in his and she was meeting his eyes. I listened for a bit; she was trying to tell him just to wait but he wasn't havin' it. If his boys had any stones they'd already have tried to get me out the hard way. But they was waffling even as he tried to tell them to come get me. Win put her hand on her hip and walked out saying she was going to get hot water and they were going to wait. She had a tell though. She let her fingers slide across his just a bit too long. Looked at him a little too soft while her other brushed her belly.

"That's when I knew what the whole of the story was. So, I pulled the curtain back and walked between the toughs. Told 'em I decided I smelled good enough. I walked out and found Win at the fire and told her I had changed my mind. I asked her if they was married and she got mighty nervous. Tried to clam up but I calmed her down. She says they ain't wed, but they are lovers. Says Chinese ain't allowed to marry any but Chinese. That true?"

Ying didn't answer.

"Ying that girl's with child and scared. I got to thinkin' those boys with the neck scars might be the problem. I asked her and she clammed up again, but it was clear enough when she glanced across the street. Told her I'd take care of it, but she almost passed out with fear. Said they couldn't know. So we worked it out. I told her they wouldn't know and that if she had trouble she could find me here. Then I made a show of being angry about my bath and stormed off. Boys followed me all the way back, probably outside now. Gotta admit I'm tempted to go out and stomp their asses.

"I also gotta admit I wasn't sure I should tell you. I only just decided I would a minute ago.

"I don't know what kinda rules you all got here Ying, but I ain't gonna be happy any harm comes to that girl or her child."

His eyes locked on Old Ying's. The room seemed to vibrate with a tension that I could barely understand.

Ying nodded and said, "You have my word, Mr. Wasco, it is for that reason I sent you. I will tell you if she comes to call or is in need of help."

Wasco stared at her a moment longer, nodded, and made a sound like rocks grinding.

"Okay," he said. "Cost me a haircut and trim and a bath I ain't even get. Hope it comes to something good."

"I believe it will, Mr. Wasco, and you look much better without the rat's nest of a beard. Probably should have stayed for the bath though," Ying said.

Wasco scowled. I let out a breath I didn't know I was holding and I saw Li's body relax.

"I have one more service I could use your talents for Mr. Wasco. Christopher and I were working on a tincture for a customer and it turns out I am out of the Neguri root I need. She knows what it looks like and where to get it, but I am afraid it is not safe to send a young girl, even one such as her, out of the gates alone. Would you be willing to escort her out, Mr. Wasco? It is only about half a day's travel to the Edge where the plant grows. There can be dangers, even this close to the city. I would send one of the young men, but none of them knows this particular plant."

Wasco looked at me.

I shrugged and said, "Ain't no worse than here."

"What about your ma and pa, they okay with you running out in the wild?" he asked.

"Pa's dead s' far as I know. Ma's doing a shift down in the mine. Won't be out 'til the end of the week," I said.

"Your ma is a miner?" he asked.

I looked at him like he was daft. It was becoming a habit with him.

"She's a whore, chucklehead. She works the mines. They don't let women be miners. She usually works six days at a time down there," I said.

Old Ying looked sad and I felt her hand scrunch down the curly ball of my hair and pat my head. I didn't know why

Ying always got that look. It was just what it was to me. Ma seemed happy enough with her lot and had been able to feed us.

Wasco and Old Ying exchanged a look.

"Okay, yeah, I'll take her out. She's a tough kid, she'll be fine," Wasco said.

"You can leave tomorrow. I'll have Li set up a pallet for you to sleep on if you like. Christopher, will you be staying here tonight or going home?"

I looked at Wasco. "A tough kid you owe a nickel to," I reminded him. "I'll stay here if that's okay?"

CHAPTER THREE – JACOB

I watched the sun rise through the constant fog that covered the rest of the Chinese Quarter. I didn't know why I woke up so early. I usually slept as late as I could, but there I was, wide awake, looking out the small window. I picked up the nickel Wasco had given me and bounced it across my knuckles.

I used to take Ying's medicines to old man Cranston who had shown me how to do that nickel trick before he died. I'd been the one that found him. Took some medicine over from Old Ying like I always did and found him dead in his chair. I don't remember being sad, which is odd because he was always very nice. Used to give me candy.

I decided I might as well get up and see if there is anything to eat before everyone else got up, so I put the nickel into my vest pocket and climbed off the pallet Ying had made for me.

I padded through the shop, looking at some of the new items, finding comfort in those that had been there since the first time I set foot in here with Will. I ran my hand across the case that contained a familiar book. *The Red Book of Hergest,* Ying had called it. She always liked to tell me stories from it when I had been little. Truth be told I wished she would have kept on, but I would never have admitted to such a thing. I walked through the curtain to the kitchen, trying to be as quiet as I could. I need not have bothered.

Wasco and Old Ying were already at the table, the Chinese fire rifle leaning against the trapper's leg. He held a wooden mug of what I assumed was coffee by the smell while Old Ying sipped her tea from a ceramic teacup. There was a plate with a few pieces of biscuit, a crock of honey, and butter on the table.

"Mornin' sunshine," Wasco said.

"Why are you up so damn early?" I asked him then nodded towards the gun. "You buy that already?"

"We need to get moving girl. Don't wanna be out all night." He nodded at the rifle. "Ying wants me take it out with us."

I sat down. "Nothing but damn crumbs left," I complained.

"Shoulda got up on time," Wasco said.

"You ain't say a time! 'Sides, how the hell does a body know to just get up if nobody wakes 'em up?"

He grinned.

"Pigheaded mrphmphh!" the words dissolved into the biscuit crumbs and honey I stuffed into my mouth.

Ying didn't keep horses, so we set out on foot toward the gate. Wasco wanted to go past Keaton Industries on the way, so we took the long way 'round to the gate. Keaton Industries sat on the west side of Edge City, right up to and even over the cliff, with rails and buildings built right into the side of the wall. The winds blew from the west, so all the steam was blown away from it and right into the folks in the Ends. A few years earlier they had raised a tall picket fence around the place with little guardhouses.

It was something between a fort, a plantation, and a mining outfit. Keaton himself lived there in a house overlooking the expansive operation. Mine workers and whores went in from the End side where all the barracks and warehouses were. A large rift separated the work area from the main house. It was like a giant axe had cleaved into the cliff face and left a gash that would not heal. A narrow bridge spanned its width.

Wasco didn't say anything. Just stood there looking for a few minutes, turned, and walked off.

We walked a few blocks in silence, which wasn't unusual from what I had learned of the large man. When he spoke all of a sudden, I about jumped out of my skin.

"When I lived here this was just a small town. Wasn't no Heaven or factories. Just this part of town you call the Ends and only 'bout half of that. Miners called it the End of the World. Weren't no steam either."

"You used to live here? And it weren't no city? How old are you?" I asked.

"Old," he said. "But not that old. This just kind of popped up. Musta been fast."

"How could you have been livin' without seeing a city being built?"

"Was up in the mountains," he answered.

And that was that. I tried to ask more questions, but he just walked and grunted at them once in a while.

The gate was just north of Keaton's place. There were guards, but they didn't pay no mind. Hadn't been much fighting with Natives in a while; the Red Legs were the most aggressive of them and had not been seen in a few years so the guards mostly slept.

We walked out the gate and headed back southwest along the city wall. Most of the traffic was coming in. Farmers and ranchers with their wares for sale or to buy supplies. Some people were heading out, but by the time we turned to the west we were alone.

After a couple of hours with no talk I got bored and took out my spitshot. I dropped a Blackchip through the hole on one end of my shot. As we walked I looked for something to shoot. A few feet off the trail ahead a long-eared hare lifted its head and sniffed. I stopped and hockered up a good ball of spit. That drew Wasco's attention and he stopped and watched me. I placed the end of the root into my mouth and let fly with a ball of spit that hit the Blackchip. The root collapsed where the spit hit it and the chip shot out in a puff of steam. The hare hopped, flipped, and landed on its side twitching and making mewling noises. I just missed the head and it got the neck. I ran over, told it I was sorry, pulled my little knife, and killed it quickly. I tried to wipe my tears before Wasco could see, but I could tell he noticed.

"I'm the best shot in town. I hardly ever miss. I hate it when they suffer is all!" I said glaring at him with tears glistening in my eyes.

"Ain't nothin' wrong with that girl, way it ought to be. You sent it along as fast as you could. We can eat it."

I looked at him sideways. Can eat it? What hell did he think I killed it for? I tied it to my belt.

"What's that thing you shot it with?"

"Oh, it's a spitshot. Usually I can knock one in the head with it, so it doesn't suffer," I said.

"What the hell is a spitshot? Lemme see that?"

He put his hand out and I handed it to him.

"You ain't never seen one? It's a spitshot, it shoots Blackchips." I pulled out a handful of small black stones from my pocket.

"What's a Blackchip?" he asked.

"Old chips that are too used up to power things anymore. People just toss 'em out, but they usually got a little steam left in 'em. If you get 'em wet, they make a little burst of steam. Well, you gotta break 'em first usually," I said.

"How come it don't burn yer mouth with steam?"

"Drinker root." I held my shot up. "Don't tell me you ain't never seen a Drinker tree?" I asked.

"Yeah, I seen 'em."

"Well, if you cut one of the roots off, a good straight one, and ya spit into it, it does the same thing it does with the tree. It closes. Go 'head. Spit in it."

He did. The root collapsed and continued to constrict the entire length until pumping the spittle out the other end.

"See?" I asked. "That way the steam can't go backwards and get into your mouth. Well, mostly. When they get too old they quit workin'. Wyatt got a good ole blister when his quit workin'."

"Huh."

He looked it over and handed it back. I stuck in another Blackchip in case I saw another hare.

The ground was sloping down slightly, and we could feel the edge of the cliff. You couldn't see the cliff edge because of all the growth, but you just knew it was there. Maybe it was the lack of trees in the distance or something in the air changed, but you could just tell when you're nearing a cliff like that. The hill was covered in all kinds of plants. I spotted some Neguri plants right away, so I figured we would find a good haul.

We found a good spot to set up and Wasco started a fire and cleaned the rabbit while I went to gather some of the root. After an hour or so I had my bag full and my belly was grumbling. Wasco had some rations he dumped into a pot with the rabbit and I scrounged some wild carrots. It made for a decent stew that we sopped up with some of the biscuits Wasco had not bothered to tell me were left.

"So, what you got against Keaton?" I asked.

He looked at me but didn't say anything.

"You got a murder'n look when you saw that loudmouth's badge and again today at the mines," I said.

"One of them boys took my Bella while they were out rustling horses. I aim to get her back."

I waited to see if he was going to continue, but he didn't say anything more and the look on his face didn't invite more questions. We finished the stew in silence then spent the next few hours finding and digging out more Neguri roots. They were spread apart, but there were a lot of them, so by the time we finished, the day was mostly gone. It would be long past dark by the time we got back.

The sun was setting before we were halfway back, and the wind had picked up. The temperature dropped, and I was shivering. I hadn't thought about how cold it was outside of the gates or I would have asked Ying for a cloak or something. He didn't say anything, but Wasco altered our path a bit. It kept us in the trees which blocked some of the wind and would be a shorter, if more difficult, walk, but the extra exertion also helped keep me warm.

Another hour or so had passed when Wasco stopped suddenly, and I bumped into him because I had my head down from the chilly wind.

"Come on! I'm cold!" I said.

Wasco held up a hand. I assumed that meant to be quiet and I was too cold to argue so I shut up.

"Heard something. Gonna go check it out," he said.

He walked into the trees; well, it was more like he became part of the trees. He barely made a sound, even crossing dried leaves. Every time he stepped his foot was carefully placed. Sometimes he would set it down, stop, lift it, and set it somewhere else, feeling something I couldn't hear, I suppose.

I didn't know why I didn't try to follow him. He had a way of making me act out of sorts. He hadn't told me not to follow him, and any other time in my life I would have. Maybe it was because he didn't tell me not to. Instead I just stood and watched him disappear into a copse of trees while I shivered alone in the darkening night. A long time passed before he reappeared, as if he had always been there waving me toward him, putting a finger to his lips for quiet. When I reached him he bent down, talking quietly.

"Somethin's happening on the other side of these trees in a gully down there. Not sure what yet, but it ain't good. Somebody was down there fightin' like Kilkenny cats. It's gone quiet now, but I need to get closer to see what it was."

He locked his eyes on mine but didn't say anything else. A shiver ran down me, you know, from the cold.

"I ain't gonna just sit out here freez'n!" I told him through chattering teeth.

His eyes wrinkled, and he flashed a rare grin.

"I figured." he said, "Come on, try to move slow. If somethin' starts to give underfoot, stop and move your foot aside slowly. Ain't no need to hurry, whatever happened is done."

He turned and started through the trees again with me following. I tried to emulate his movements the best I could. If I was too loud or if I succeeded, he gave no indication at all. I stepped in his foot falls when I could. I think I did a passable job. We came out of the trees and Wasco hunkered down as he climbed a small ridge and knelt at the top. I moved as slow as I could, just like he had, and followed him up. I think I saw a slight nod of approval, but it might have just been what I wanted to see.

"Okay, ain't no cover 'twixt us and them now. You gonna wait here if I tell ya to?" he asked.

I couldn't get up the nerve to say no, so I just shook my head.

"I didn't think ya would and I ain't sure that'd be all that smart anyway. So, I want you to stay right behind me the whole way, understand? No matter what. Even if someone shoots at us, you stay directly behind me, got it? Ain't nothin' here you need to see or do," he said.

Shoots at us? Who was going to be shooting at us? What the hell was I doing? But there was no time to think or ask because Wasco had turned and was heading over the ridge, trying to find whatever shadows he could. The moon was new and the sun had set, so at least it was mostly dark.

Nobody shot at us and we made our way down a rocky slope. I smelled the smoky remains of a fire, and something else, something tangy on the air. Metallic tasting. We stopped, and Wasco turned and told me to wait while he looked around. We were next to a covered wagon with a broken wheel; I didn't see any horses and didn't hear anything. I had been so intent on staying right behind him I hadn't even noticed the wagon until we were against it.

He took a few quiet steps out and around the wagon and stopped. He turned back and looked at me with a look I'll never forget. It froze me in place.

"Do not come around this wagon, understand me?" he said in a harsh whisper. "Don't look; don't even come close to this side. It ain't pretty out there."

The look in his eyes, even in the dark, would have stopped a charging bull. It was a command. A law that was not to be disobeyed, and that was the problem.

I wasn't able to respond with words looking into those eyes, but I knew what I was gonna do. He gave me another hard look to reinforce the command, turned, and crept back around the corner of the wagon.

He hadn't gone ten steps before I was peeking around the wagon. There were bodies lying all around a burned-out fire pit, steam rising from dark pools of blood in the cool night.

"What's the big deal, he think I ain't never seen dead people?" I mumbled to myself. "Seen more than he has, I bet."

Me and authority have never mixed all that well. I didn't like being told what I could and couldn't do. I damn sure wasn't going to let some red-leg juniper boss me around.

At least that's what I told myself right up until I got close to the first body. It was lying in a way that didn't seem natural even in the darkness. It was twisted up all wrong. But that wasn't the worst of it. It had been mangled and looked to have been partially eaten. Most of its face was missing, and he looked to have reached for his gun. I could tell because I stepped on the severed forearm that ended in a hand holding a steam pistol. I made a sound I don't think I could ever make again, covered my mouth, and ran back to the safety of the wagon.

It wasn't enough. I needed to go home; I needed away from here and from Wasco. I was panicking. I needed to run as far from there as I could and never look back. I was preparing to do just that when Wasco's heavy hand touched my shoulder. It was gentle, but the weight of it was like a mountain that held me in place.

"I told ya girl. You shoulda listened," he said sternly. "But ya can't just run off into the dark 'cause you saw somethin' ugly. There's a lot of ugly in the world and runnin' from it… well there ain't no future in that. Ya might just run right into worse."

His eyes held me as much as his hand did, but not in the commanding way from before. It was something else, something that made me feel safe. The look in those eyes got my feet on firm ground again.

I took a breath.

"I'm fine," I said and tried to pull my shoulder from under the weight of his hand. But he held me still with a gentle squeeze.

"What?" I asked. "You think I was scared? I just didn't think I'd step on a damn... I thought it was a snake or... I'm fine!"

He looked at me for seconds that felt like they lasted a day and a half and nodded his head.

"Yeah, yer fine. Let's get out of here. Ain't nothing to do fer any of them anyway," he said.

"What happened? Why are they all dead? Did something... something ate them didn't it? A bear? Could it have been a bear? Why didn't they shoot it?"

I was still shaken, and my words were just tumbling out, so I didn't hear the groan that came from under the wagon. Wasco did. He spun, rifle coming up as a man crawled towards us.

"Damn Red Legs! I told you to run!" the man said.

The voice was weak and dry sounding.

Wasco just looked at him. The man got to his knees and looked up at us, eyes squinting in the darkness.

"Wait, you are not them. Why are you... did you kill them?" he growled.

He started to stand. Blood covered his mouth and torso and he was naked. Very naked. I should have been embarrassed.

He looked like he was about to leap at Wasco and attack him with his bare hands and took a stumbling step forward. At some point I must have pulled out my spitshot since I noticed it was in my hand. Before I had time to think, I had raised it to my mouth and hockered into it. A jet of steam propelled the Blackchip out and it hit the man right in the chest. It wasn't enough to kill a man, it was just a spitshot, but it packed a wallop and hurt like hell. I'd been shot with one before. The man fell backwards, landing hard on his back, limbs going akimbo. Wasco looked at me, at him, then walked over and put the barrel of the rifle in the man's mouth.

He said, "I ain't killed nobody son. These men was dead when I got here and there damn sure weren't no Red Legs around. So, what the hell are you doing here and why are you alive when they aren't?"

As he talked he swept his arm to indicate the mutilated bodies. It made me look too and I swooned. Wasco caught it.

"Girl, move over there so you can keep yer eye on him."

He pointed with his chin to a spot that would make seeing the bodies difficult.

"Gewrl?" the man said trying to talk around the gun barrel.

He moved his eyes over to me, looked down to his naked body and tried to cover himself with his hands. A push with the gun barrel stopped him. He looked around and tried to motion with his eyes at the wagon.

"Mah cloves are im vere," he mumbled.

"What?" Wasco asked and moved the barrel back a bit.

"My clothes are in that wagon. Might I get some trousers on, since you brought a little girl with you?" he said.

"Anything else in that wagon we might wanna know about?" Wasco asked.

The naked man shook his head.

"Alright, I'm gonna back up a step and you're gonna stand up real slow, understand?" Wasco said.

He nodded, and Wasco took a step back. The man slowly climbed to his feet.

"Topher, go look in that wagon, but be careful, don't go jumpin' in before you look," Wasco said.

I stared at him.

"Come on girl. I need you to fetch them."

"I ain't no dog!" I said and crossed my arms. "I don't fetch!"

"You damn sure ain't! Dog's listen better" Wasco said. "And they're a mite friendlier too! Now can ya git in there and grab this man's things so he can cover his danglers? I'm gettin' damn tired of lookin' at 'em."

I stomped over and climbed into the wagon throwing a glare toward the man, daring myself to not look away.

"And make sure there ain't no weapons!" Wasco called.

The only things in the wagon were chains with manacles attached to them, and a pile of clothing with a pair of guns in a gun belt sitting on top of them. I looked through the pockets of the trousers, pocketed some coins and a pocket knife before I tossed them out, followed by the shirt, boots and undergarments. When I climbed back out carrying the gun belt, the man was pulling on his pants. He buttoned them and picked up his shirt.

"Might as well tell yer tale before you put that on. No sense in me putting a hole in a nice shirt if I don't like what you got to say," Wasco said.

The man looked up from his shirt, over to me holding his gun belt, then back to Wasco.

"Can we sit?" he asked.

"You start talking while we walk out of here." Wasco waved the barrel of the fire rifle up the way we had come. "We'll see if you live long enough to sit."

"Fair enough," the man said.

He picked up his boots and started walking up the rocky hill.

He was a handsome man. Muscles flexed and moved over his stomach and chest as he climbed the hill. His longish blond hair blew over an angular face with sharp eyes. Where Wasco was made of stone, this man was made of knotted

41

linen. His movements were fluid and confident even while he marched up a hill at gunpoint carrying his boots and shirt. When he spoke, he wasn't winded at all even though we were all struggling against the loose rock.

I was so distracted looking at him that I jumped when he started talking.

"My name is Jacob. I was trading with a band of Red Legs Natives when those men charged in. They were on us before I could even draw iron. Chained us like animals in that wagon. I do not know where they were taking us. They stopped to set up camp and something attacked them. I got the chains open and told the Natives to run. I tried to follow after I got free, but something hit me in the head. I woke up to your voice and saw your red pants. I thought you were the Natives at first and wondered why they hadn't run. My head was still muzzled. My next thought was that you might have been one of the bandits that had taken the pants as a trophy. Why are you wearing the pants like a Red Legs anyway?"

Wasco didn't answer right away, just kept walking up the hill, eyes on Jacob.

"Why were you so worried about some Natives?" Wasco asked.

"I have an understanding with many of the People of the Nations. It requires I do what I can to help them when I can," he said.

Wasco was quiet for another hundred paces.

"I wear 'em 'cause I am one, well half anyway. Mother was of the Nations, Pap's a scoundrel. So where you headin'?" Wasco asked.

"I'm afraid I do not know where I am, so I'm unsure where to go from here, but I would prefer to not go there without my pistols. Or my boots on."

"Give him that belt Topher," Wasco said.

"What? Just like that? How you know he ain't lyin'?" I asked.

"I don't." He looked at Jacob. "I trust they'll stay in them holsters."

The look was convincing.

"Yes, they will," Jacob said, meeting his gaze and holding it a moment before pulling his shirt over his head. "Mind if I stop to put my boots on?"

Wasco kept walking. Jacob stopped, brushed off his feet and pulled his boots on, and jogged to catch up.

"Got any water? I'm a mess."

Wasco pulled his water skin from his belt and tossed it at Jacob who caught it. I assume he caught it anyway, because his hand moved so fast all I saw was him suddenly holding it and popping the cap off.

"Where are we headed?"

'Headin' back to the End of the World," Wasco said.

"Edge City you mean?" Jacob asked.

A noise rumbled from Wasco that seemed like it might be agreement but sounded more like the beginnings of a rockslide.

Jacob didn't stop talking the whole walk back. He splashed water and wiped away the blood on his face and chest as we walked and stopped a couple of times to dump rocks out of his boots. Wasco by and large ignored him but asked a few questions here and there. Jacob said he was a sell gun, meaning he'd work for about anyone that would pay him. Judging by the money I had taken out of his pocket that wasn't many people, so I figured he wasn't that good. By the time we made it back to the city, Wasco had hired him, said he could use another gun to back him up when he confronted Keaton.

The wooden chimes welcomed us back to the shop with their song and Ying met us at the door.

She stood in front of the door blocking our path for a long couple of breaths, eyes on Jacob.

"He's gonna be signing on with me for a job. Jacob, this is Ying."

Jacob bowed low at the waist in the same way Li did with Ying. She did not move right away, but eventually she nodded appreciatively and returned the bow.

"It has better manners than both of you," she said and walked away with her cane tapping along the floor.

Jacob, for his part, looked a little too proud of himself if you ask me. Wasco stared hard at her retreating back before glancing at Jacob, brow furrowing. Ying went through the curtain to the little table. When we joined her Wasco told her what had happened, and they squared away their dealings for the rifle. Ying invited them to stay in the stockroom until Wasco had concluded his business in the city, for rent of course, which he could pay when he was able. That was as far as I heard because I was exhausted. I went back to the little mat Ying had for me and was asleep in minutes.

I woke up after breakfast the next morning. Wasco and Jacob were drinking coffee and talking. Ying was reading a book and I could hear Li in the shop getting ready to open for the day. Thankfully, Ying had saved me some breakfast this time, so I stuffed my face.

Wasco counted out the few dollars he had left and slid them to Jacob.

"Ain't gonna get any easier, let's go," Wasco said.

He stood up, slung the fire rifle over his shoulder, walked over, and tussled my hair.

"Yer a tough kid," he said.

"Whatever chucklehead," I returned.

He did that thing that passed for a smile and walked for the door with Jacob following. Once I heard the door slam I counted to ten and got up to follow them. I expected Old Ying to stop me, but when I glanced her way she just kept reading. It was odd, but my youthful ignorance insisted it was none of her business anyway. There was no way I was going to miss Wasco charging onto Keaton's place.

Wasco and Jacob were about twenty paces up the street looking at me as I slipped out the door.

Jacob reached into his pocket and handed a coin over to Wasco.

"Come on," Wasco said, "I knowed you was gonna come anyway."

He turned and continued walking. Jacob waited and watched me run up, grinned, and we headed after Wasco.

CHAPTER FOUR – KEATON

It wasn't hard to spy on the Keaton Company. It was a huge complex on the brink of the massive cliff that gave Edge City and the Ends their names. The cliff was the result of a curse the Native tribes had put on the land a hundred years before. It blew a hole in the earth hundreds of feet down that spanned hundreds of miles. It was called the Edge of the World because it created a towering wall between the west and the east.

It wasn't supposed to have created such destruction I'm told, it was just meant to drive away the white invaders that had arrived decades before. Red Coats and Blue Coats who had been fighting over who got to steal land the Tribes had lived on for centuries, at least that was how the Natives saw it. So, they gathered in a great conclave and their shamans made a curse that would drive the invaders away by making the land unproductive for a year to anyone whose ancestors were not buried here.

What many do not know is that some of my ancestors from Africa were also tied to the Spirits of Life and knew the feel of the magic, even if it was at the time, foreign to them. They had priestesses who heard the call of the Native Shamans and added their power to the curse when it was cast. My people had been slaves. They had been brought from

Africa and were angry and lonely, and missed their land. The magic they added to the spell was the magic of sadness and of anger, and retribution.

It caused a massive backlash of energy that left the Edge of the World dividing the continent in half. But there were always unintended consequences. The explosion uncovered earth that was not meant to see the light of day. Earth that held veins of Ember that Keaton discovered almost a hundred years later. That discovery fueled a new wave of white invaders calling themselves "The Enlightened," and the resulting industry poisoned the land below the Edge with the spreading blight we call the Blacklands.

"That's them, I'm sure of it. It was just like that one there," Wasco said.

A medium-sized ship lifted off the ground, its side bladders full of steam. It climbed by jetting steam out the back. When the sails unfurled, the logo featuring the "K.I." of Keaton Industries was painted clear and large.

"Ya think?" I said. "Keaton's the only one that's got'n flying ships for a thousand miles. Who else would it have been, chucklehead?"

Jacob snorted, and Wasco gave me a look.

He handed me back my pa's old spyglass he had borrowed and I took a peek at the ship. The men were running around working levers and ropes. I wondered what it must be like to be up so high. Of course, I had climbed out O'Donnelly's branch over the Blacklands before, so it was probably like that. A tickle in your belly that makes your legs want to go weak.

"Ain't no sense wastin' time. Gonna go down and have some words with the Keaton."

With that Wasco stood up, grabbed his new rifle, and started down the hill.

"Wait! Yer gonna do what? You been done brown if you think you can just walk in and have words with Mr. Keaton just like that. Ain't not a body in the Ends even seen him in years. You don't even know if he's in there! I hear he got hurt in the mines, so he don't like ta be seen."

"Well, there'll be somebody down there will know where Bella is," he said over his shoulder. "Let's go Jacob, time to earn them dollars."

Jacob looked at me and quietly asked, "Who is this Bella anyway and why would she be down there?"

"I think it's his horse," I said, and jumped up to follow Wasco, who was down the hill and onto the street.

He was like a stone rolling down a hill. He wasn't going fast but seemed to gain momentum the closer he got. Jacob and I were a few steps behind him by the time he reached the gatehouse. A guard stepped out and asked if he could help us. When Wasco didn't stop he said more firmly that workers and applicants needed to use the east gate. Wasco walked right by him.

I will give the man credit; he only took a second to react after his surprise before he found his courage. I'm not sure I would have, given the look on Wasco's face. Then he made a mistake. Instead of calling for help, he ran up and grabbed Wasco by the arm.

Jacob and I stepped over his prone body. He wasn't unconscious but wasn't getting up anytime soon either. He just sorta looked around blankly with blood running out of his nose from where Wasco's fist had hit him. Jacob let out an impressed whistle. Wasco kept walking, making a beeline for the big house on the hill, where I 'sposed he figured he'd get his answers.

It only took maybe two minutes before someone figured out what was going on, rang a bell, and mustered some men to try and head us off. Three men in uniforms stepped out in front of us, hands on steam pistols. Another in fancy clothes stood off to the side of them, hand near his own pistol. Nobody drew their guns, and Wasco's rifle was still slung over his shoulder. I guessed that was good but I started looking for a place to run anyway. Wasco stopped and eyed them.

"Gonna have to ask you to put that rifle down and step away from it," Fancy Pants said.

Wasco just let his gaze go to each man, lingering for a moment before moving to the next. Jacob stepped up beside him, his hands easily at his sides. Nobody moved. Seconds passed like hours. The tension was a physical thing. Jacob flexed a finger that made an audible pop.

I jumped.

So did the guards.

"Holy shit, Snake? That you?" One of the guards pointed, "That is Jake 'the Snake' Watson right there. I thought you was dead out in the Nations?"

"Nope. Not dead. You sure you want to be standing there with your hands on them pistols like that?" Jacob asked.

Two of the men moved their hands far away from their guns. The other and Fancy Pants didn't. More day-long seconds passed with everyone just standing there. I heard the sounds of people shouting somewhere behind me, a bell ringing in the distance, and general commotion. It felt like I was outside of it all, just watching. But I wasn't. I was right there, surrounded by men with guns that wanted to use them. I started shaking and would have bolted if I hadn't been so scared of being shot if I did.

It was Fancy Pants that moved first.

"I said drop that rifle, now!" and his hand went to his gun. It might have cleared two inches or so of leather before there was a loud clap of gunpowder pushing lead. A little spray of blood hit the dirt in front of Fancy Pants. Another followed, and another.

In a steady rhythm, his heart pumped his life out through the hole in his chest. He landed in it face-first. Jacob was standing there with a gun in each hand, one trailing smoke, the other trained on the guard that had kept his hand on his gun. I hadn't even seen him move. His guns were just...there.

"Come on guys, he's just one guy. Shoot him!" the man said, hand still on his pistol.

"I don't reckon I'd do that," Wasco said.

He hadn't moved, not even a finger. Rifle was still slung over his shoulder. But he may as well have been pointing a canon at them given the reactions of the two other men.

"I ain't nowhere near ma gun, mister."

He was looking at Wasco, afraid even though it was Jacob that had just killed their boss. His eyes did flick to Jacob and back again, though.

"Burt, that's Jake 'the Snake' Watson and this devil of a man gots the look of death all over him. You want 'em shot, you shoot him! I got a wife and kids at home and I don't get paid enough to go against the Snake and a devil," one of the men said and backed away.

It was a chilly morning, but sweat still ran down my back. Another year passed in seconds while we stood waiting to see if anything was going to happen. I think I'd have pissed myself if I'd have had anything to drink earlier.

"There is to be no more shooting, Mr. Conner. Mr. Keaton will see to it from here."

The voice came from my left and I about jumped out of my skin. It was an old man with skin darker than mine. He was dressed to the nines, looking like he was God's butler.

"Mr. Watson is it?" he looked to Jacob. "If you would be so kind as to put those away, I shall show you directly to Mr. Keaton and you may air whatever grievance you might have."

Wasco eyed him and said, "Works fer me. Put 'em away Jacob. Come on girl," he said as he walked past me.

Jacob grinned a fool's grin at the guards and slid his guns away. I expected some kind of fancy flourish and spinning, but he just dropped them in, tipped his hat, and followed us.

The house was a castle; or might as well have been anyway. With two sweeping staircases leading to large wooden doors in the center of a massive porch. Marble columns held the roof of the porch up, dark wood framed all the windows. I had never seen anything like it. I had seen the house from far outside the gates, but up close it seemed to go all the way to the sky.

"This place is huge, it's bigger than all the houses I ever seen put together!" I said.

I could not stop looking up even though it was making me dizzy. I couldn't even imagine how someone could get to the top of something that big. Wasco and Jacob seemed less impressed, but Jacob did let out a whistle as he took it all in.

The butler led us up the left staircase and onto a porch my house could have fit on twenty times over and held the front door open for us. The house was as amazing inside as it had been from the out, filled with things that reminded me of Old Ying's shop. The floors were all white marble, and it looked like the furniture had never been used. The butler led us into what he called *the pahlar* and told us to wait. Wasco leaned against the wall, Jacob sat and put his feet up on a table, and I slipped a nice looking silver spoon that had been sitting in a bowl of some kind of seeds into my pocket.

"Yer mighty fast with those," Wasco said to Jacob. "But 'Jake the Snake'? Little dramatic ain't it?"

Jacob pinched some of the seeds from the bowl with his fingers and chewed them, giving me a wink.

"I didn't make it up. One of the guys I used to run with did. It just kind of stuck. Back then I wasn't even that fast. We all just thought we were and gave each other stupid names like 'Snake' and 'Sidewinder' to prove it."

He nodded toward Wasco's rifle. "You don't shoot that thing much do you?"

"When I do, it'll be 'cause I need to," Wasco answered.

"You didn't think you needed to against four guns back there?"

"That's what I brung you for. 'Sides, it was only two guns, any fool could see them other two weren't gonna draw," Wasco said.

Jacob gave a short laugh. "No. No, they were not."

We waited and waited more. Wasco got madder than a hornet and was about to storm off to find Keaton himself when the butler returned.

"He will see you now, please follow me."

"'Bout damn time"

"I am sorry, Mr...?" He looked at Wasco expectantly.

Wasco stared back.

"He wants to know your name mush-head," I helped.

Wasco gave me one of his looks and Jacob choked on some seeds.

"Wasco. Name is Wasco Foley. This here's Jacob and Topher," Wasco said.

"Thank you. As I was saying, Mr. Keaton was in an important meeting. He was not expecting you. Had you made an appointment I assure you he would have been prompt."

He turned and motioned us to follow. Jacob made a face mimicking him as we trailed him down a hall with a fine red rug over hardwood flooring that didn't creak. Soon the butler stopped and pushed a button on the wall. I heard a grumbling noise and a few seconds later he slid a part of the wall open and motioned us into a small room. Wasco and Jacob both stopped outside. I walked right in and looked around. On one wall there were three levers and a knob I was getting ready to turn until a glint of metal in the corner caught my eye. Kneeling I picked it up and looked it over. It was a triangle-shaped button with intricate designs on it. I gave it a bite. It was real silver, so I slipped it into my pocket with the silver spoon. This was turning out to be the best trip I'd ever taken. I could eat for a year with these — if I could sell them before someone stole them from me. Meanwhile, Wasco had that look again and he and Jacob were refusing to step in.

"What the hell is this?" Wasco asked.

"It is a lift sir. It will take you up to Mr. Keaton's office on the fifth floor."

Wasco made his stone-on-stone sound.

"Okay. Then, you come too."

He pushed the butler in and stepped in behind him.

"I had intended to, Mr. Foley. I need to operate the levers. If you'll excuse me."

He maneuvered around Wasco and pulled the door shut. Once it was closed he pushed one lever up and the next down. I heard the sound of steam and the floor lurched.

"What the hell!" the three of us shouted.

The butler eased one of the levers back slowly and I felt the floor go out from under me a little. He reached over and opened the door. What had been a hallway was now a large room with a man sitting behind a desk. There were couches arranged on the walls opposite him and a large set of oak doors behind him.

"Mr. Wasco Foley, Jacob Watson, and Ms. Topher to see Mr. Keaton as he requested."

The man nodded, pushed something on his desk and repeated our names into a small horn or something.

"Send them," came the scratchy reply.

The doors opened into paradise. At least that's what it looked like to me. Everything was white and gold and dark wood. There was a fountain right there in the house! With fish in the pool, their colorful fanned tails spreading out behind them as they swam below a gold cage full of songbirds. The far wall was a window of the clearest glass I had ever seen. I was able to see all the Ends, with the steam rolling along in little clouds that crept up from the Edge.

To the right I could see the great dark expanse of the Blacklands stretching for miles hundreds of feet below. It looked like a giant ink stain on the earth. In the far distance were the mountains that marked the end of the Blacklands and the start of the Nations. Through the other window I could see some of the houses in Heaven that were right at our eye level. I had never been able to see any of the actual houses before, and although they were far away, their opulence was evident. As I watched the tiny people moving through the streets I couldn't help but wonder what it must be like to live here. It was a mesmerizing view. I knew I would never forget it.

"You appear to have some manner of grievance with me or my men," the man behind the desk said. "Do you wish to discuss it and come to terms, or shall we continue with the shooting? You have already killed one man I am told. I am willing to overlook that if there are to be no more."

I admit I had been so enthralled by the trappings of his wealth I had not even noticed the man behind the desk until he spoke.

Mr. Keaton, because there wasn't anyone else it could have been, sat behind a giant wooden desk. It was not messy, nor was it perfectly ordered. On the corner sat a melon-sized chunk of translucent green Ember with the skull of some sort of animal trapped in it.

He was dressed in a brown suit and white shirt, wore a scarf, gloves, and hat. Most strange of all though was the mask he wore that covered his whole face. It seemed to be made of wood carved to look like a stylized skull, like the ones I had seen during parades. It wasn't grotesque or overly done, it…well, it kind of fit.

From behind it his voice sounded hollow and forced. Like there wasn't enough air to make the words. I looked up at Jacob and he had the same open-mouthed expression I imagined I did. Wasco, of course, was unaffected. He walked up to the desk crossed his big arms and stared down at the man in the mask.

"One of yer flyin' boats took somethin' that belongs to me. I want it back. Maybe with a pound of somebody's ass fer my trouble."

"You are Mr. Foley I presume? My name is William Keaton. I do not know what it is you are speaking of, but if one of my men stole from you, I will make immediate restitution and may in fact allow you the requested pound of their ass. And that will pale compared to what I take for it costing one of my men their lives. But first, I will need more details," Keaton said.

Wasco was silent for a few minutes. I think he was confused about why he wasn't stabbing or shooting someone.

"Happened up in the mountains. One of your ships come along makin' a hell of a racket, firing off guns to beat all, chasing some wild mustangs. My horse spooked and bolted before I could get to her. Got caught up in the mix of the stampede with all my gear tied to her but the pelts I had just retrieved. They landed, and a couple of your boys rode off and kept up the chase while the ship dove down into a valley. They looked like they was gonna run them right off the cliff, but that ship of yours came up right at the edge and they ran 'em right into the open doors. Ten or so wild ones and mine!"

Wasco looked down on Keaton who was tapping a finger on his mask in what seemed to me to be a thoughtful manner.

"I think I know what happened to your horse, Mr. Foley. If you will sit for one moment, I will explain."

The two locked stares for some long seconds before Wasco nodded and took a chair.

"Go ahead I'm listening," he said, "but first, any reason you wearin' that get up?"

"Ah, I should have explained. I forgot you are not from the city. Most people in Edge City know I was injured in a mining accident many years ago. I am afraid my visage is not very pleasant to look at, so I give it my best effort to not scare small children," Keaton said and nodded my way.

"I ain't small. I'm at least nine," I told him.

He looked back to Wasco who shrugged.

"I believe it was one of my ships that took your horse," Keaton said.

"I already knowed that."

"But it was not anyone from my company."

"Bullshit, I already know yer the only one that has flyin' ships. I ain't gonna sit here while you shovel manure onto a plate and call it dinner," Wasco said, starting to stand.

Of course, he only knew that 'cause I had just told him an hour before!

"That is true. I am the only that owns flying ships. Mostly. But not long ago one of my ships was in fact stolen, and by a man that is quite capable and likely to be acting the way you describe. I had heard he might have taken it to rustle horses and cattle. You now confirm that," Keaton said.

Wasco looked unmoved. But Wasco always looked unmoved.

"Think about it, Mr. Foley, does it seem to you I have need to wrangle horses? Do you truly think I would risk an enterprise that has changed the world and made me what I am today to wrangle some horses? Were the men who gave chase to the horses in uniforms as all of my men are?"

"Yer makin' some sense, keep talkin'," Wasco said.

"I have been told a man that calls himself Bull McCain has my ship, and therefore has your horse, or at least knows who took it. I would like to offer you a bounty Mr. Foley. One that will solve both of our problems and make right what I am in a small way responsible for. Find this Bull McCain and my ship. I will pay you and Mr. Watson each five hundred dollars if you will locate and free it from the Bull's possession.

"If yer ready to throw so much money at a man and you know where it is, why ain't you just sent yer men to get him?" Wasco asked.

"The few I've employed have failed at the task and other recruits have been, hesitant.

Wasco cocked his head, eyes narrowing.

"This Bull McCain and his gang hold up in the Blacklands, Mr. Foley," Keaton said.

Wasco grumbled and looked over at Jacob who gave him a nod.

"Sure, I'm in," Jacob answered.

"Sounds reasonable to me. Makes sense even. Maybe too much sense. But I can't fly no ship and got no desire to."

"You need not. Simply locate where it is, free it from his possession if you are able, and lead a crew back to recover it.

"What about this Bull McCain, what do we do with him?" Wasco asked.

"I simply do not care, Mr. Foley. I want my ship back; he has had it long enough and is damaging my reputation with his rash actions. If he is unable to be a bother to anyone again, I say good riddance."

"Alright, you got yerself a deal."

"Excellent," Keaton replied. "I will have Hanson prepare a small advance and the necessary paperwork."

Wasco started for the door. Jacob put his hand on my shoulder and gave me a shake to snap me out of the spell that giant window had me in.

"Come on kid," he said.

"Gentlemen," Keaton's hollow voice called from behind us.

We all looked back.

"The Blacklands has many dangers and I am told many strange things happen there. Please tell me you do not intend to take a small child there?"

"I ain't no small child, pig knocker," I informed him.

Wasco just shrugged and walked out the door.

CHAPTER FIVE – OLD SHIT

I spent the entire walk back to Old Ying's alternating between trying to figure out how to convince Wasco to let me go with them and being terrified he might. The Blacklands? Nobody with any sense went into the Blacklands! I knew some bad types did, but not normal folk. I looked over at Wasco and Jacob and realized the reason I wanted to go is that they weren't normal folk. Not even close. It was hard to put my finger on it, but they both just had - a presence.

I felt like being around them would lead to something I needed to be a part of. They were like Keaton's big window. They gave a glimpse into the wider world. A world I only thought about when Old Ying would read to me.

It started raining about halfway to Chinatown. I didn't mind, even if it was cold. I liked the rain. It washed some of the stench off and drove the steam back for a bit. I still hadn't come up with a good way to go with them, short of sneaking out to follow when the Chinese Quarter came into view. I knew my ma would be coming up from the mines soon and there was no way she was going to let me leave the city. Definitely not with two men as old as my pa and I couldn't even imagine what she would say about the Blacklands! I couldn't just disappear while she was home though. All too soon I looked up to see the glass window of Ying's shop.

She met us at the door and I knew something was up right away. Something in her face even before she said, "Come in out of the rain. Close the door tight behind you. Christopher, we have much to discuss."

Wasco took off his coonskin cap and shook out the water which got him a scowl from Old Ying. Jacob took notice and stepped back to the door to do the same with his wide-brimmed hat outside. Ying started dabbing me off with a thick towel.

"Li, put on some tea and coffee," she called.

We all sat around the little table in the back and warmed our bones with tea and coffee. Nobody said anything for a long time.

"Christopher, I received a letter with news from your mother," Ying said.

Damn! She would want me home right away, and I hadn't figured out what to tell her!

"She cannot leave the mines for another week. There were some, issues. She asked that I keep an eye on you, so you will be in my charge for a while."

"I ain't never had nobody be in charge of me before when she works. I ain't no baby!" I said.

Jacob's grinned across the table and that set me off even more.

"What are you grinnin' at you damned flat!" I shouted at him.

Tears were starting, and I hated that. I wasn't sad, I was mad! But that's the curse of being a woman I guess. Cry when you're mad, when you're happy, cry about damn near anything. But it made me even madder. Ma I might have been able to fool into letting me go, but not Old Ying. I was never able to get over on her!

"Christopher, your mother asked this of me and I must honor her request, as must you. She is worried because they will not tell her when she may be allowed to leave, but it will be more than a week. I will escort you into the Blacklands with Mr. Wasco and Mr. Jacob."

I was too worked up to even notice what she had said, but Wasco and Jacob's heads snapped up to look at her, startling me.

"Ying," Wasco said, "I'm gonna need ta ask how you keep doin' that."

"Doing what, Mr. Wasco?" She met Wasco's gaze and did not waver.

Wasco made that sliding rock noise again and just kept looking at her. Jacob cleared his throat. I took the opportunity to wipe the tears off my face and snorted to stop my nose from running.

Wasco spoke first, "When I first comed here you knew my name before I ever said it. Topher hadn't said it either. But you called me by my name just the same. Now we just sat down and there ya go, knowin' what we had to do without even a word between us. That's edgin' a might past odd."

"Mr. Wasco," Ying said, "if we are to take this journey together, it is high time we put our cards on the table, do you not agree? I am more than an old lady running a curiosity shop, as you already know, and you are more than the mountain bumpkin you pretend. Mr. Jacob," Ying looked Jacob in the eye, "well he has a story to tell as well. Surely my knowing your name and guessing what is to come does not seem so strange in the context of the things you have seen in your life? You and Mr. Jacob know a bit more about these things than you let on, do you not?"

Jacob looked away, chewing on a matchstick. Wasco stared hard at her, and then he settled back into his chair, never breaking eye contact.

Wasco was first to break the silent staring contest.

"I reckon I do at that. So, how's that bring us to you and Topher here goin' into the Blacklands? That makes as much sense as tryin' to saddle break a cougar"."

"I am still capable of managing a hard trip, Mr. Wasco, and I will have Li with me as well, to look after my needs. My skills at healing are not insignificant, and I expect I will contribute in other ways as well. There are things that will need done out there that guns alone will not solve. One of those things is that this girl is going into that place with or without our permission."

All three of them looked at me.

Ying said, "You were going to try and follow them, were you not, Christopher?"

She looked back to Wasco.

"Since I have known this girl she has done nothing that makes me think she will be less stubborn and strong willed about this than she has anything in her life. As I have been given her charge, it is my duty to make sure she does not go without me. So, we are in agreement. When shall we leave?"

I had not known Wasco for long, but I was pretty sure few people had ever set him back like Old Ying did. He just sat there, almost looking mollified.

"We should leave soon," Jacob said as he turned to look at Wasco. "Those men, the ones that you found me near, I heard one of them mention someone named Bull. It did not dawn on me until now, but that seems an awful bit of a coincidence. We left without searching things. I think we should get out there and see if they had anything that might help us before the crows and coyotes get them."

"Reckon so. How about mornin'?" Wasco said looking at each of us in turn.

I certainly wasn't going to object, gift horses being as they are and such.

Wasco said, "Topher, I know yer a pigheaded girl and like to think you know a lot about everything, but this place we're goin', it ain't like nothin' you ever seen. It's dangerous, and don't even start to open that mouth of yours, you hear."

It wasn't a question and I had been about to mouth off. But he had that damn look on me again, froze me like a scared rabbit. God, I hated that!

"Now listen good. It ain't just strange, it's deadly. You could die out there, and there won't be nothing left to bury if ya do. I wouldn't have none of it if I didn't know Ying was right and yer dumbass would be sneakin' out after us anyway. So, you gonna have ta swear to me that you won't gimme none of that bullshit of yours. One of us tells ya to stay put, you stay put; we tells ya to be quiet, you be damn quiet. It ain't no game and it ain't cause yer a kid neither. It's 'cause I been there before, and I know what I'm talkin about. It's that or I swear to God I will tie you up and leave you in the closet."

I nodded my head.

"No, goddammit, you gotta say it. Say you swear you'll do as you're told!"

Oh, how I hated him. I felt hot tears roll down my cheeks again. I was shaking. I was scared of him. I was scared of going. I was scared of not going. But mostly I was mad as hell. I just sat there shaking with tears streaking my face.

"There's more," he said voice softening a bit. "I'm gonna swear also. I swear that I won't be treatin' ya like no kid either. If yer gonna go out there, yer gonna be a full-on equal. Even get a cut of the pay. This ain't about me thinking yer a little kid, kid."

He looked to the others and back to me. "I ain't sayin' this because yer a kid or a girl. I'm sayin' yer one of us, so yer gonna have to act like it is all, and I swear I'll treat you that way and get you back home alive." His granite hand reached out and covered my tiny black hand and squeezed gently.

"I ain't gonna treat ya like a kid."

That broke me. I sobbed, and my walls came crashing down. I swore like he'd told me to. Up to that moment nobody had ever talked to me that way. Like a person. An equal. My ma loved me, that was for sure, but she didn't know me. She had to work too much since Pa had gone, and I had been growing and changing alone. Will and the gang didn't really know me either. They still treated me different because I was a girl. Wasco was recognizing I was truly part of a group.

Nobody hugged me, because that wasn't what I needed just then, and they knew it. I needed to work out how I felt being outside of my walls. I sobbed while they talked about details. When the subject of my carrying a gun came up I lifted my red but tear-free eyes.

"A rifle," I said. "I can't hold a pistol when it goes off, but I can shoot a rifle."

They all looked at me, but nobody asked how I knew how to shoot. I was glad I didn't have to explain about us taking Samuel's dad's guns and going shooting. I never thought it had been worth the whoopin' we got, but I guess it was now. That was a few years ago, but by my age most of the boys that lived outside the city handled rifles and even some in the city when they had to travel with their families. It was only because I was a girl and my pa was gone I didn't get trained to shoot.

"All right, can ya ride?" Wasco asked.

"I don't think so. Ain't never have," I said.

"Ok then. I'll get a mule fer ya. You can ride that easy enough and we ain't lookin' to set a blisterin' pace."

I wanted to protest and yell about how I wasn't no addle-brain that couldn't ride a horse, but we had moved past that. Saying it would just seem childish. I'm sure I caught the corner of Wasco's mouth twitch in a slight smile when I didn't challenge him.

We didn't get on the road until close to noon the next day. Wasco had picked up a couple of horses and mules for us. It was a warm late-winter day with the sun out in a cloudless sky. A breeze was blowing so there was hardly any steam at all.

I named my mule Old Shit, because it was old and shit brown. Wasco rode a dappled Appaloosa and had traded his coon skin cap for a wide-brimmed, tan hat with a rounded top. Jacob had a black horse with a white diamond on its head and wore his black Stetson. Li rode on a small brown pony and Ying had a mule like mine. Li was wearing some kind of armor and had a sword and bow tied to the side of the horse and both he and Old Ying wore those pointy straw hats I had seen around town. Wasco moved his horse near me and tossed a small box at me.

"Yer gonna need that out there or the sun'll eat you up. I tried to find somethin' you could fit all that hair under but gave up and grabbed one I thought you might like."

I opened the box and took out a hat. It was black with a not-too-wide brim that was flared up on the sides. The crown flared, like a coachman's hat and it was flat on top. Around it was a leather band with silver disks attached. I pushed it down onto my head. It fit nicely; I had no idea what it looked like on me, but it felt nice.

Wasco grunted and rode back to where Jacob was.

"It is a perfect hat, look for yourself," Ying said and held out a mirror with a pearl handle.

She was right. I don't know how that gruff old fool did it, but it was the only hat I could imagine on top of my cloud of curls.

We rode single file with hardly a look back. When we reached the gate, I thought I should look back, that this was some momentous occasion in my life, but I didn't really feel it. I was just trying to convince myself I should. So, I rode out of Edge City without a backward glance.

Outside of the city the air was crisp, and my cheeks quickly chapped. The breeze that had been pleasant inside of the city walls was a rough wind out here. I can't put words to what I was feeling as we rode through the gate. I had been outside of the city walls many times, but not like this. This was different. I wasn't coming back tonight, or even tomorrow. I would be sleeping outside in the Blacklands! I wasn't afraid; I was too young to know I was supposed to be. We are all immortal as children.

By the time we got to the copse of trees near where we had found Jacob, I just wanted to be out of that dammed saddle. My ass hurt, my legs hurt, my back hurt, and I was bored out of my mind. When Wasco put his hand up and slid off his horse I was pleased to hear him groan a bit. I jumped down with the energy of youth and fell right over. My legs had completely forgotten about standing, let alone jumping. Jacob put his hand out and gave me a lift.

"Should have warned you about that. It'll take some getting used to," he said.

Nobody laughed and my embarrassment passed quickly.

Wasco said, "That was yer free one kid. Jacob falls like that he's gettin' a line a shit thrown his way. I figured I'd let you settle in before we started in on you though."

He gave me a friendly shove that made me stumble and I laughed.

"Ok, let's go, but quiet," he said. "Remember how I showed you? It's get'n on in the evening so there are lots of shadows. Try and keep to them. Place yer feet quiet and follow me. Got no reason to think there's anything at all down there, but ya never know."

He looked a question at Ying and she nodded. He disappeared into the trees. It was almost magic the way he blended in. I was right on his heels and it seemed like he was a ghost. Ying and Li, who hadn't said much of anything the whole trip, weren't as good, but they were quiet. Jacob was not. He just walked, his hard boots crunching leaves and branches. I don't even think he was trying.

"What in the hells are you about?" Wasco said.

He had stopped and was staring at Jacob like he was a loon.

"You tryin' to make sure we let everything fer a mile know we're here?" Wasco said exasperated.

Jacob looked sheepish. "Sneaking isn't something I have much practice at. Why don't you go ahead, and I'll wait here till you give me an all clear?"

"Chucklehead," I said and stuck out my tongue as I walked past him mimicking Wasco's movements.

When we reached the ridge-line Wasco waved his arm down hard and we all dropped to our bellies and froze.

"Topher git back and tell Jacob to get up here as quiet as he can but to stay low, if they look up here they might see yer heads," he said in a whisper.

Just the day before, I would have thrown a stubborn fit about being bossed around. Now I hurried back, being as quiet as I could, feeling proud he had given me the job.

Jacob wasn't quiet, not by a long shot, but he moved slow and stayed hunched over, crawling the last fifteen feet to Wasco who was on his belly, rifle in hand. We slithered up next to him and peeked over.

"I count eight of 'em. Look like road agents, could be Comancheros. Snake, what'r you thinkin'?" Wasco asked.

Jacob looked at Wasco. "Are you really going to start calling me Snake?" he asked.

"What, ain't you 'Jake the Snake' no more?" Wasco asked deadpan.

Jacob just rolled his eyes.

"I don't think they are either one," Jacob said after a minute or so. "They are loading the bodies onto the wagon. Why would agents or Comancheros bother to take bodies?

69

And look at their guns. New model steam rifles. Pistols look the same. Road men don't carry weapons like those."

Below, the men had replaced the broken wheel on the wagon and were tossing the last of the bodies onto it. I felt the acrid taste of bile as I remembered the half-eaten, twisted corpses. Thankfully, I was too far to see them clearly and I was not about to reach for the spyglass.

"Looks, like they've got them loaded. They're getting ready to head out," Jacob said.

Wasco made his gravely grunt as he sighted down the rifle.

"Keep yer heads down," he said.

Jacob looked over at him. "That's got to be close to two hundred yards with a cross wind. Be lucky if you can hit the side of the wagon from here."

The wagon started to move. There was a bang and a flash. We all watched for something to happen. I could make out the men frantically looking around as the sound echoed around the bowl of the canyon and one of their horses reared up unhurt. It seemed as if he had missed everything. Wasco rolled over to his back, tucked his head down, and started reloading.

The driver of the wagon snapped the reins and the horses leapt forward. Some of the men had steam guns drawn now but none had spotted us yet.

"Just keep yer heads down and wait," Wasco said.

He sounded so confident, but it seemed all he had done is let them know we were there from what I could see. The wagon lurched, turned to the left, and rolled to a stop. The horses kept running on.

"You have got to be kidding me!" Jacob said.

Jacob sighted down the slope with the spyglass and made a low whistle.

"You hit the damn yoke of a moving wagon in the wind at near two hundred yards?"

Wasco grunted. "Yoke's the part still on them horses. I hit the tongue."

Meanwhile the men below were looking this way and that with guns out.

"Gonna be needin' ya to leave that wagon and ride on!" Wasco called over his shoulder.

Wasco's call echoed off the hills a couple of times. The men jumped and renewed their efforts to find us.

"You ain't got no claim to it!" one of them called back.

"Just ride away boys. Ain't nothin' there worth getting killed over, got rifles on ya all the way round!" Wasco called back.

Wasco was already done reloading the rifle. I had never seen anyone load a muzzle loader that fast.

"How about I come down and talk about it. Hold yer damn fire and maybe we can make a deal. Tell yer boys to find leather for them guns, I'll do the same. Anyone pulls 'em and yer the first that's gonna get a bullet!" Wasco yelled.

Without waiting for a reply, Wasco said, "Alright, Jacob, take Li there and see if they'll trade him for the wagon."

"What?" Jacob and I both exclaimed at the same time.

"Got any better ideas? Now I'm thinkin' you know how to use that pigsticker you got there Li. And Jacob here, he is mighty fast with them pistols. So, he'll take ya down there like yer his prisoner and be holdin' yer stuff where you can get it. When shit hits the fan, you start stickin'," Wasco said.

"How am I gonna draw my guns if I'm holding his stuff?" Jacob asked.

"Drop it," Wasco said.

Jacob stared at him.

"So, you figure I'm going to stand there in front of eight armed men, wait until Li grabs a sword, drop what I am holding and draw before they do?" he asked.

"Yup"

"I can do that," Jacob said ginning.

"What should I do?" My voice was shaking. I was petrified he was going to tell me I would have to shoot someone.

"We're gonna have two of our own down there and you ain't been shootin' long enough to risk shooting into that. You seen me load, can you do it?"

"I know how ta load a damn rifle!" I snapped.

A voice came rolling up from below. "Alright stranger, we holstered them, come on down and we can talk!"

Jacob peeked through the spyglass. "Nobody's holding."

"I knowed ya could," Wasco said, looking me in the eye. "Just needed to make sure you can do it when there are bullets in the air. I'm gonna shoot this round and hand you this rifle, you hand me yours. Load it and be ready to trade again, got it?"

I nodded my head but wasn't sure I could get my hands to stop shaking.

"And keep yer head down!"

He looked a question over to Ying.

"I will do what I can," she said.

He made that rocky sound and nodded.

"Okay, Jacob and Li move down off the ridge a bit and get ready, walk out around the rim a bit before you head down so they don't eyeball us. Tell him we got Li and some other runaways and need to get them to the rail to get paid, but lost our horses to the Rot and had to leave the wagon. See if he'll trade that wagon for Li."

Wasco pointed with his rifle, "I'm gonna hit the first one that goes for his gun. Him being on fire is your signal."

Li slid soundlessly off the ridge followed by a less-quiet Jacob. Wasco scowled at him. Li gave his sword, bow and arrows to Jacob who wrapped them in a blanket loosely and mock tied Li's hands behind his back. It took some doing but eventually they were arranged so Li was practically holding the hilt of his odd-looking sword while Jacob held the scabbard and his bow and quiver wrapped in a bundle of clothes. They headed off and around the ridge. I held my breath.

I tried to watch for them to come around the bend and watch the men at the same time. I was making myself dizzy whipping my head back and forth. Eventually I caught sight of them making their way down the rocky slope into the bowl of the valley. Jacob had his hands out in front of him and would occasionally shove Li forward. He stopped when one of the men raised a hand. I couldn't make out the words, but the muffled sound of their voices echoed up to us.

"Sounds like they're buyin' it so far. Get ready," Wasco said.

"How do you know they won't just take the trade?" I asked.

"I don't. Been wrong before," he answered.

"But what are we gonna do if they take Li! You sent him down there and you don't know?" My voice was edging onto hysteria.

"Quiet girl. I ain't wrong this time. See there. Watch the guy in the straw hat. He's movin' his horse to get out of Jacob's line of sight," Wasco said.

He leveled the rifle and took a breath. I jumped from the flash and bang. When I looked back down the hill the man was on fire. He dropped to the ground, dropping the gun he had drawn and started rolling around screaming. Someone must have caught sight of us because bullets began to whiz angrily over my head. Wasco shoved the rifle at me and grabbed the Winchester from my numb hands.

"Load girl!"

My hands started moving while I peeked between the rocks. Li had grabbed his sword and leapt toward the man in front of him, two quick movements and the man fell, in at least two pieces. I swear Jacob's guns had appeared in his hands before the bundle he dropped hit the ground. I heard a crack I thought was one of Jacobs's guns, but the sound split when it echoed from the walls to reveal it as two simultaneous shots.

One man fell from a horse and didn't move again. Another grabbed his arm, yelled, and backed behind a large rock. Wasco popped up, fired three times with the Winchester and two more men fell. Ying pulled a small clay vial from her apron and worked the cork out of it. She said something into the bottle and took a drink without swallowing. She puckered her lips and blew out gently. A seemingly endless rope of mist flowed from her mouth and down the slope like a serpent. When it reached the horses they all spooked and kicked and jumped. Two men ran from behind the panicked horses and Wasco shot one of them. The mist reached the other and wrapped around and up him like a giant snake. When he tried to scream the mist flowed into his open mouth and he simply fell over soundlessly.

I stared at the scene and whispered, "What was that? Did you kill him?"

"A spirit of the wind," was all she said.

Wasco tossed the Winchester back to me and grabbed the one I had just loaded. I forgot to load the Winchester and just held it, mesmerized by the scene. Jacob and Li were stalking the wagon where two men were taking cover. When they tried to make a run for it, shooting as they went, Jacob filled one full of lead and the other fell with an arrow in his chest from Li.

Just like that it was over. It had seemed like hours, it had only been seconds since the shooting started. Wasco stood up and headed down the slope.

"That coulda went worse I suppose," he said.

I was getting up to follow when I heard the *hiss bang* of a steam pistol go off. Wasco fell forward, hit the ground, rolled, and then slid a few feet down the rocks, a black stain spreading on his chest. I spun around, and the man's steaming gun moved over to me, his bleeding arm held tight against his body. It was the guy Jacob had wounded, he must have snuck away during the fight and came around behind us.

CHAPTER SIX – MOVERS

"You just sit tight right there boy. Toss that rifle over, that's right, nice and slow," he said to me.

I tossed the Winchester towards him. I shoulda been scared, but I wasn't. I was numb.

"Old woman, get over here by the boy," he said to Ying.

He called down the hill, "I got your woman and the boy. The big man is dead. I'd say we can do some talkin' now. Lemme hear those pistols hit the dirt."

He was looking down to Li and Jacob trying to see over the ridge and not paying us a bit of mind, thinking me just a child, and a boy at that!

I don't remember what I was thinking when I did it, I just remember being mad that he kept calling me a boy! Before I knew what I was doing I had pulled my spitshot from my belt and hockered into it. He spun back toward me at the sound and the Blackchip hit him right in the eye. His gun went off. He dropped it, grabbing at his eye, and fell to the ground squirming in pain. Lights exploded in my vision and things went blurry. He rolled over to his dropped gun. For an instant my vision cleared, and I watched as he grabbed the dropped weapon and came up pointing it at Ying. Warm blood flooded my vision, the world turned sideways, and I was falling.

Darkness. I could hear a buzzing around me and I tried to swat at it, but something was holding me down. White hot pain as something tried to dig into my skull. I kicked, screamed, and gnashed my teeth, but I could not get free. It felt like a boulder held me down. I fought harder and let loose every swear word I'd ever heard, but it was useless. Things cut, prodded, and poked into my skull. Something was wrapped around my head tightly, squeezing it. It stuck to and pulled at my skin.

I thought about the spiders I'd heard stories of that would creep up from the sand to wrap sleeping people up in their webs and eat them alive. The spiders were burrowing into my head and I knew I'd be eaten from the inside. I wondered how long it would take to die. When would the pain stop? Something vile and sticky poured into my mouth and I tried to spit it out. Pinpoints of light flared in my vision and the pain slowly receded to a dull pressure. The buzzing started sounding like words, like someone calling my name. I wondered if it was God calling me to Heaven. I hadn't ever thought about God before, but Ma talked about Him all the time.

I opened my eyes and was blinded. It was so bright. As my watering eyes cleared, a face appeared lit from behind by a glowing ball of fire. There was something protruding from it, like a handle. Then everything snapped into focus and I was staring at the face of the bandit split by a Native axe, blood running from the wound, sun setting behind it. I let out a squeal and tried to roll away, but a hand pushed me down gently and held me fast.

"How 'bout you just lay there a minute or two kid. Bullet grazed your noggin; luckily, that's the hardest spot on ya. I don't think it did nothin' more than knock ya silly for a bit," Wasco said.

He was looking grim-faced down at me. My ears were ringing, and I could barely make out the words.

I reached up and felt a bandage wrapped around my head. I felt the warmth of blood under it and a knot the size of a walnut and I swooned thinking of spiders.

"How? I thought you was dead," I said.

"It would probably hurt a lot less if I were, but nah. Passed right through and missed everything important. I oughta be alright, same as you, now drink the rest of this," he said.

He pushed a clay vial to my mouth and tipped it too far for me to do anything but swallow or drown. Good thing too, it was the vilest stuff I had ever tasted. I couldn't begin to describe it or I'd wretch in the thinking. Suffice it to say, it was not something I wanted to ever drink again. Too bad for wanting I guess. Once the taste was gone though, I felt the coolness of it flow through my body. Immediately my head felt better, and the burning, throbbing pain stopped. It itched like someone had wrapped it in poison ivy! I reached up to scratch it, and the bump was almost gone. I felt around, and it didn't hurt too touch.

"One a Ying's mixes," Wasco said. "Fine stuff that. You nap a while; you'll be good as new when you wake up."

I couldn't keep my eyes open. Darkness crept in from the sides and I learned something. Wasco was a damn liar.

"Ah shit!" I yelled waking up. I wrapped my hands around my head. It felt like it was going to burst.

"You said I would be good as new! I'm dyin' you mother lovin' son of a bitch's bastard's whore!" I swore.

I was sure I invented a lot more swear words before the pain subsided with the help of another of Ying's potions, and I should have felt guilty. I didn't. Damn but my head hurt.

After another nap of indeterminable time, I woke up to the crackling of fire. Ying was lying flat on her bedroll and I could see the silhouettes of Jacob, Wasco, and Li sitting on logs around a fire, talking quietly.

"What happened? Where are we?" I called, my voice sounding strange to my ears.

"To answer the second question first, we are in the same place, more or less."

Li's voice.

I half scooted, half crawled over and leaned against the end of the log.

I looked to Wasco, "I thought you was dead. He shot you. Did he shoot me?" I reached up to touch my bandaged head.

There was no bump and no warmth of blood. Just an itchy scab.

"Yeah, he did. Shot us both. Just didn't shoot us dead thanks to you and that peashooter, and Ying's concoctions," Wasco said.

"Peashooter? My spitshot? Oh yeah, my spitshot! I shot him with it then everything went dark!"

Wasco nodded then said, "Ying says when you spitshot him his gun went off and grazed yer head. Lily-livered sumbitch had come 'round the side and shot me in the back. Bullet missed the lung, but it knocked me on my ass. Wasn't ready fer it. When I got my head back on I looked up and he had his gun pointed at Ying. I had dropped my rifle, so I grabbed my hawk and threw it. Split his head."

"Ying? Is she…?" I asked hesitantly, afraid of the answer.

"She's fine. He missed her clean," Wasco said.

I let out the breath I didn't realize I had been holding and realized that my bladder was set to burst.

"I need to piss," I said and started to get up. "Is it safe? To go out there?"

"Yes, it is safe. Over by the horses I got a hole dug. Here," Jacob said, and he handed me a lantern.

When I returned, Wasco was talking.

"So, I joined up to fight the Empire, think I was round 'bout fifteen years old. Wasn't for any noble reasons though. I was just full of piss and vinegar. Couldn't stand being in one place all the time. Life with Natives before they sent me off, it had been different. We moved all the time. When they dropped me at my sister's place things were different. They stayed in place, never going more than the mile to town. So as soon as I was able I joined up with the Union.

"Fought fer better part of a year. The last battle, it was nasty. Things had changed toward the end. The Union was tired, and that made them do things that were hard to settle with. But the Empire, those Enlightened sons a bitches, they were ambitious. And that'll make men do worse." He took a breath and continued.

"Battle of the Mississippi was a long, bloody affair. The Enlightenment had been workin' with steam-powered suits. Big suits made of all metal they'd pump full of steam with hoses. But they couldn't really control 'em. They would just charge into lines of men, their arms swingin' with abandon, killin' their own as much as they was killin' us. They didn't care.

"They sent African troops in with them, to throw water on the metal suits. To keep 'em cool I think. Most of the black troops got burned so bad they got left behind or stomped into the dirt by the damn thing they was throwin' water on." He made that noise in his throat. "And that weren't even the half of it. End of the battle came, and we had won, if that's what ya call all that blood and all those bodies. I was done. I picked up my pack and my rifle and just started walkin'.

"Walked all the way back to Endtown. It was just a lil' Podunk place then but there were still too many people for me, and I couldn't rest easy in one place. So, I kept walking right up into the mountains and I hadn't walked out till a few days ago."

"That's been what? Thirty years? You mean you missed the last thirty years in the mountains? You didn't see the steam cars or know about Ember?" Jacob asked.

"I guess I kinda knew. I'd see a thing here or there that would seem a might strange, but when yer living that close to the Blacklands you see plenty of strange things. I hadn't really known what it all was till Topher here showed me."

"How did you get so burned up?" Jacob asked. "When Old Ying was working on you I saw your chest. You have scars all over."

Wasco met Jacob's eyes then slid his gaze to me. "That wasn't from the war. That there is from the Black Rot," he said. "That's what all of ya better be knowin'. The things that live where we're goin', they ain't just strange. They're deadly. Some of 'em are sick with it and they can give it to you. Can even spit it at you. And it ain't like other wounds. It'll pus up and ooze out and eat ya from the inside."

He rubbed at a spot on his side. "My second year in the mountains I hadn't really knowed about the Rot yet. I was out hunting and saw what I thought was a black bear. Turned out to be a Rot infected brown. I took the shot and hit it square, but it didn't go down. Just turned and came at me. I loaded and fired again but it still came on. I killed it by chopping it to pieces with my hawk, but I got plenty bloody in the process. Silver Owl, Shaman of the local tribes, was able to clean most of it out, but some of it needed burned out. I wasn't supposed to live through it. It was better than dying from the Rot, which the tribes say kills the soul and the body."

Jacob said, "I've seen some fellas with the Rot, it is not pretty. Painful way to go."

Wasco nodded. "Yes, it is. Not everything in the Blacklands has got the Rot, but enough does. It can't hurt me no more, so you let me take care of 'em if it comes to that, you hear?" he locked gazes with each of us.

"We ain't got no shaman to cure it," he said, "and you wouldn't survive their *care* if we did."

Those words held in the air for a full minute. Then Old Ying's voice, quiet as a mouse on goose feathers, came out of the darkness.

"I can cure the Rotting and will not kill you. But still we must heed Mr. Wasco's warning. I can only do so much."

I thought I was ready enough to ride by morning, but everyone said we needed to rest a bit more, so I fell back to sleep and slept like death. Between Ying's concoctions and his constitution, Wasco looked like he hadn't even been shot, except the hole in his shirt and coat, and an occasional grunt when he moved his arm. That man was made of stone, I swear.

The following day we set an easy pace, leaving the bodies burning in the wagon behind us. Wasco and Jacob had searched them while I was out, and found a wallet with some papers, sure enough spelling out a bounty on prisoners and bodies signed by Bull McCain.

The next night's sleep was all I needed to feel right as rain and the following day felt like we were just out for a Sunday ride.

"Why would a horse thief pay money for dead bodies?" Jacob asked.

"Been wonder'n on that myself," Wasco said.

By nightfall we had reached the cliff edge and the trail that led down into the Blacklands. Ying was standing at the edge of the cliff looking off into the distance. I joined her, and we stood there together for a long time not saying anything. The sun had just left the horizon and was lighting up the west in purples and pinks. A dragon soared on the wind, silhouetted by the falling sun.

Ying said, "In my country we consider dragons to be noble and wise creatures."

"They're just flying rats. Eat dead stuff," I said.

"I suppose that is partially true for some. But they are legendary in China. I suspect even out there, they are far more than flying rats. Have you seen one up close?"

"Na, they don't come near town cause they get shot at I guess. Ma says they used to, but people killed 'em."

She reached over and pulled the spyglass from my belt and held it out to me. "Look closer," she said. "See if you see more than a flying rat."

I took the glass and searched the sky, remembering to move slowly. It had settled on the air currents and was just hanging there in the air. It was not at all what I had expected. At first it appeared to be black and completely covered in scales that almost looked like feathers, and then it caught the waning light in prismatic waves of color.

Its wings were spread out and even, though it didn't seem to be going anywhere, and its serpentine body undulated through the wind. It fanned its tail out and I gasped. It was covered in feathers that presented a glorious display of color. Green and red and purple, even gold. It waved it back and forth in rhythm with its twisting body and I couldn't move, couldn't breathe. Then it folded it in, tucked its wings and dove for the ground. I pulled the glass away from my eye to try and locate it again. That's when I saw the other one diving behind it in pursuit.

"A mating call. That's what the tail is for," Ying said. "Males call the females with that display. We are very fortunate to see such a thing. It is a good omen."

I watched the horizon, trying to find them again.

Ying patted my head and walked back to the fire. I stood there as the light faded, hoping for a last glimpse of the dragons. Just as darkness swallowed the last of the light I thought I saw them or one of them, anyway. I would never know for sure but I think it had the other one hanging limply from its jaws.

I walked back to the camp and settled into my bedroll thinking of the dragons. How could it have been so beautiful?

As the darkness deepened it brought with it a pervasive feeling of dread. Something wasn't right. I sat up. Nobody was asleep. Every rock and tree seemed to be hiding some danger. While nothing threatened us, I didn't sleep one wink that first night. Come morning everyone but Wasco looked like they hadn't slept either. If Wasco had or not I couldn't tell; he was the same as he ever was. He moved around, stowing gear and packing horses. If he noticed the rest of us were dragging ass he made no mention of it. He did the work that was usually done by us all without complaint. We eventually climbed into saddles and made for the trail that would take us down into the Blacklands.

It was not much of a trail; it wound down, hugging the wall of the cliff on the inside. On the outside there was a fall hundreds of feet. I was not happy, but Old Shit didn't seem to notice. He was a dumb old mule, but he was surefooted as could be. There were a few places where we had to get off our mounts and walk them single file because the ledge was too small.

"We won't make it down before the sun sets," Jacob said.

The sun in question was about a hand span from touching the horizon and we were no more than halfway down. I had been dozing in the saddle and started awake at the conversation, almost falling, which put my guts to twisting.

"There's a place little further down. Need to pick up the pace a bit though," Wasco called back.

It was dark by the time we found it. Riding a mule on a ledge a hundred feet up in the dark was not fun, of that I can swear. But surefooted Old Shit never faltered. *It* was a small cave in the side of the wall. Wasco went in with a lantern. There was firewood stacked against the back wall with some crates and a cask. Wasco went over and exchanged some of the wood he had gathered above and started a small fire.

With the night had come that same feeling of dread. The blessing was that none of us had really slept the night before, so I just threw my bedroll out and went to sleep, too tired to care if something was coming to eat us.

I woke up to the morning sun and tried to blink the glare away. A Natives face peeked around the corner of the cave and I screamed. The face pulled back and let out a yelp itself.

Wasco said something in what I assumed was the Native language. He had his rifle trained on the mouth of the cave. The Native's face reappeared.

Wasco said something else in the Native tongue and the man smiled slightly and stepped out with his hands in the air.

They talked back and forth for a bit, clasped hands, and the Native headed down the path toward the Blacklands.

"Was he tryin' to sneak up on us?" I asked.

"Nah, he was gonna take his rest here on his way down but saw us, so he slept out on the ledge. Got here a little after we did and didn't want to alarm us."

"He alarmed the hell outta me," I said.

"Yeah, well yer an excitable girl," he said with a grin and started stoking the fire.

I said, "Yer a pain the ass."

Once the fire was going he said, "He did gimme some direction. Said he's been seeing movement due west, thinks he saw a flying ship once, but he wasn't sure that's what it was. Said there are strange things there, stranger than normal, and that he will no longer hunt near there because of it."

"Hunt? He hunts out here?" Jacob looked incredulous.

"Apache," he said. "They use the sand lizards to poison their arrows. He will tell the tribe we're here. That might be good, might be bad. Might not be anything at all, but if you see any Natives you tell me and let me do the talkin'."

The day was as much fun as the previous one had been, and I added my hands to my list of pains. I was gripping the saddle horn so hard on the way down I couldn't open them up even when we stopped at the bottom of the trail. It was only a few hours past midday, but it was already dark. Everything was dark. The sand was dark, the few plants were dark. It was like things down there sucked up the light and wouldn't let it out.

And it was hot.

Hotter than it ought to have been given the season and time of day. It was getting hotter as we descended. There had been a breeze on the trail that had died away, so I hadn't realized just how much hotter. Only a couple of things moved, and I wished I would not have noticed. A winged scorpion flew right by my shoulder and landed on a small flightless bird that looked more skeleton than bird. The scorpion started stinging it and the bird took off running, making a horrible wailing sound.

I looked questioningly at Jacob, but he just shrugged and clicked his horse into motion.

We only rode about an hour before we set up camp. Wasco had me practice shooting for an hour or so. I was okay with the Winchester, but I wouldn't be joining the traveling shows. He had me clean it and load it, shoot, reload. Shoot from one knee and lying down. From Old Shit's back and even had me roll on the ground a couple times then shoot. I didn't understand why I would ever shoot someone after doing all that, but I practiced like he said.

As the sun made its final fall to the horizon I have to admit, the thought of sleeping out there did not do any good for my nerves. I think that was why Wasco was keeping me busy all the time with all that circus shooting. We had made the camp in a cluster of rocks.

After helping clean the dishes I settled in with my back up against a rock and cleaned the Winchester. The rock was warm and comforting. I didn't know if Wasco was right about it being safe, but it definitely felt safer. I was asleep before I knew it.

I woke with a jerk and rolled forward grabbing for the gun that was still on my lap. I rolled away from the rock, tucking my shoulder just the way Wasco had made me practice, cocked the rifle, and fired. The gun flew up and out of my hands. I had not remembered to set it firmly against my shoulder. I had also neglected to set myself steady, so the kick knocked me back onto my ass. The bullet did what bullets do when they hit rock and made a whizzing noise as it spun away into the cold night.

Holding back a snicker, Jacob said to Wasco, "I told you we should have said something."

"Yea, but we'd of missed that fine shootin'," Wasco said.

"Well, she did hit it," Jacob said.

"It's a damned rock, course she hit it," Wasco said.

I sat stunned, looking back and forth at them. Ying helped me up and checked my scrapes with a frown at Wasco.

"It moved! The goddamned rock moved!" I said pointing at it.

It was still moving, ever so slowly, but it was moving. It wasn't rolling, and I could see no legs, but it was sure enough moving to the right.

"I know child. I was startled as well. I have never heard of such a thing, but they are guardian spirits and completely harmless," Ying said.

Wasco was grinning, and Jacob was trying to hide his laughter. Even Li had a sparkle of amusement in his eyes.

"Gonna put spiders in your bedrolls," I told them.

That made Jacob laugh harder, which made Li snort, which made me laugh, and before long we all had tears streaming down our faces. Well not Wasco, he did laugh though, a short deep sounding rumble, and that was as shocking as the moving rocks.

When our giggle-fit finally ended Wasco told me about the Movers. They are all over the Blacklands. Nobody knows how or why they move, but they do, sometimes gathering into groups. They have no attack or defense that I could detect, but for some reason many of the creatures of the Blacklands stay clear of the gatherings, making them good shelter for those unwise enough to travel there. Like us. After learning of them, or maybe just because I was feeling giddy after all the stress of the previous days, I felt the need to apologize to the rock for shooting it.

That got Jacob snickering again, but I swear that it heard me. That night I slept without worry and like a newborn babe. When I awoke, I found that the Mover, at least I think it was the same one, had moved close enough I could feel the faint heat it radiated. I caught Old Ying giving me an odd smile as I patted it and said thank you, but I just ignored her.

We broke camp and rode for another few hours. The morning was cold for the first hour and I was shivering into Old Shit's back wishing I was back in my bedroll next to the Mover. But as the sun got over the high sides of the canyon face it started heating up again. By the time we stopped for lunch we were all sweating in our saddles, which chapped areas best left to the imagination.

Wasco rode out ahead of us to scout things out as we regretfully climbed back into our torturous saddles. He was saying we were close to the area the Apache hunter had indicated so he wanted to get the lay of the land. The rest of us kept a slow pace following his tracks in the sand until he came back about an hour later, saying he hadn't seen anything of the bandits, but there were some odd tracks that concerned him ahead and to keep our eyes open.

We rode on with Wasco out in front, rifle in hand. I noticed Li had his odd-looking bow on his lap, arrow notched. Jacob was still unarmed, but as fast as he was that didn't matter. I pulled my Winchester out of its holster and tried riding with it for a ways. My arms got tired fast and when I tried to rest it on my knees it bumped and scraped them, so I put it away.

The rest of the day was almost boring. Nothing weird happened; I didn't see anything unusual at all. We could have been riding through the dunes west of the city, except everything had a blackish-grey coloring to it. Wasco slowed down and fell in next to Jacob and said something to him, then did the same with Li and Ying who gave a worried look back to me.

After another fifteen minutes or so Wasco said, "Ain't no rocks around and this is about as far as we can go. Gonna have to bed down out here in the open."

I shrugged. "So?"

He grinned. "Well, I guess yer right, just figured I'd tell ya there ain't gonna be no Movers around to shoot. Keep alert though, without Movers might be that a few things come 'round to see what we're about once it gets dark."

Wasco set up camp differently this time, with the horses and mules in a half arc around us, our small tent at the open side. He said he would take the first watch, then me with Jacob, and finally Ying and Li. We had never set up watches like that before, at least that I had been told. I really didn't know what it meant, but I nodded like Jacob had. The fire was small, and Wasco had dug into the sand and built it in the hole so there was very little warmth. I slept as close to it as possible. My brain tried to argue about the sleep, telling me to be terrified as the dread of the night settled in, but my body's exhaustion won out eventually. I woke to a firm but gentle shake.

"Git up kid. Need your eyes with Jacob's. Just keep alert in case any animals wander near. If you hear somethin' you wake me, understand? Don't second-guess, just wake me," Wasco said.

"Okay, I done watches before ya know," I told him.

He raised an eyebrow. "Have ya now?"

"Well, you know, in the city. When we would, um, sometimes we would play games and have to do watchin', that's all!" I told him.

I hadn't. I had no idea what I was even talking about, but I didn't want him to know that.

He nodded. "Good 'nuff fer me."

He laid on his bedroll and set the fire rifle across his chest. I walked over to Jacob.

"You think something going to attack us?" I asked him.

"I do not know, Topher. I've been out here once or twice before, but not like Wasco, never this far. Better just assume something might and keep a good watch," he said and gave my arm a pat.

He scooted around so he was looking the opposite way and I was left staring out into the dark desert of the Blacklands. Even though I knew Jacob was right behind me, I felt alone and scared. An hour passed slowly, and I was on edge the whole time. I imagined a dragon swooping down and carrying me off, or one of those winged scorpions landing on me, or a giant bear charging in, oozing black goo and mauling me.

I was getting myself into quite a state when I heard Jacob's voice. It was quiet, just above a whisper. "Are you missing home?" he asked.

He had said it so quietly, so slow and gentle, that it didn't startle me. I am sure he could tell I had been starting to shake and that was why he did it. He was a good man.

"I... I don't know. I'm scared," I said.

I couldn't believe I was admitting it, but I was too scared to act brave at that moment.

Jacob said, "Yeah, I am as well. I think we are supposed to be scared sometimes. Keeps you sharp. Makes you just a little bit faster. So long as you don't let it control you, fear is a good thing."

"I bet Wasco ain't scared," I said.

He chuckled. "Yeah well, you might be right about that."

"Did he say he fought in the war?" I asked.

"Yes, he did," Jacob said. "And he was raised by Red Leg Natives. He has got some kind of story."

We were quiet then, watching the night, but having heard his voice calmed my fears and the last hour went by faster.

When I finally laid back down after waking Li and Ying, I thought I would never get back to sleep, but again my body won out and I fell into one of those deep sleeps that lets you sleep through anything. I slept through Old Ying shaking me, Wasco kicking me, and all of the shouting. It was only the sound of the gunshot that had me leaping up grabbing for the Winchester.

CHAPTER SEVEN – SAMRAK

Around me was chaos. Everyone was moving, but I couldn't tell what they were doing. I heard sharp barks in the distance and jumped when I heard a gun go off behind me. Then Ying was at my side.

"Get up, Christopher; you need to get up now." Her voice was surprisingly calm given the chaos, but left no room for debate.

I stood up and asked what was going on. *My* voice was not calm. Over her shoulder I could see Li hobbling the horses closer to the fire and tossing some brush on it.

"Over there girl," Wasco said over his shoulder. "Get yer rifle and don't let anything get at my backside."

Wasco was silhouetted by a small ball of fire on the ground in front of him. He had turned his head to point with his chin where he wanted me to go while he was reloading his rifle. At that moment, the ball of fire climbed to its feet and leapt at him. Before I could think I levered a shell into the Winchester, pointed and squeezed the trigger. I shouldn't have. Wasco's head was right in the line.

The practice must have paid off or God was watching because I didn't kill Wasco. I did hit the thing dead on in mid leap. It tumbled backwards, tried to get up. When it couldn't, it tried to crawl toward us on its belly, black teeth bared, still burning, black goo oozing from its mouth.

Wasco finished packing the barrel of his rifle, pulled his long knife, and drove it into the canine head of the burning thing at his feet. It quit moving. In the light from the flame I could see a growing circle of blood on Wasco's shoulder. His wound must have been reopened, but he didn't seem to notice.

"What the hell is that?" I asked.

"Coyote" he said.

"It's on fire!" I yelled.

"Flaming Coyote," he said with a nod to the fire rifle.

"Why didn't it die?" I asked.

"Black Rot," he said. "And I didn't hit it clean. There's more of 'em out there. Not sure how many. Keep yer head movin' and yer eyes open."

I heard the twin blasts of Jacob's pistols behind me and ducked instinctively, almost losing control of my bladder. Hands shaking, I levered another round into the Winchester and kept looking out into the darkness, not sure if I wanted to see something or not. Old Ying didn't say anything but gave me a reassuring smile. Li was walking toe to heel around us looking out into the night. He stopped and drew an arrow back, then let fly. A faint glow traced the arrow's flight into the night. I heard a thump, a yelp, and then a thud. Li smoothly drew another arrow from the quiver at his hip and began his walk again.

A gunpowder flash and loud report echoed across the desert and another coyote was on fire and howling. I followed it with a shot of my own, but I think I missed. After a few steps it fell, then started clawing its way forward, growling. In the glow of the burning and stinking bodies I could see no less than twenty sets of eyes reflected back at me in the fire, stalking back and forth trying to keep out of the firelight.

"What do we do?" I asked. "There might be hundreds of them out there!"

Wasco grunted something I could not make out and his head snapped up, looking to my right. I didn't even see it until they went down in a tumble of claws, teeth, fists, and fur. One of the coyotes had leapt for me. Wasco, having been in the middle of reloading, dropped his rifle and jumped at it, catching it in the side and driving it away. I saw his fist pumping up and down as they hit the ground, then its teeth latched onto his shoulder and he screamed.

Another one took advantage of the opening and charged into the dying firelight, then more streamed in behind. Fear fueled my hands as I worked the lever and fired rounds as fast as I could. Then they were everywhere, running out of the darkness and trying to grab an ankle or arm, before dancing back out of the light they seemed to fear. I heard Jacob's pistols ringing out behind me, then the *click, click* of empty chambers. I shot at one, then another and another, chambering rounds and squeezing the trigger as fast as I could. Then the Winchester answered the call of Jacob's pistols with an empty *click* of its own.

Li was down to two arrows and then one, then he dropped his bow and drew his sword. Wasco was buried under a mass of teeth and fur as others had leapt on him for the kill. His stony fists crunched bodies and his grip snapped limbs, but he was getting mauled in the process. I swung my rifle like a stickball bat at one of the passing things, cracking it in the head. A commotion erupted behind me. Yelping and snarling, things tearing and breaking, then a feral growl louder than anything I had heard from the coyotes sent chills up my spine. I looked but it was on the other side of the fire and out of the firelight.

Then I was blind. The fire exploded in a huge mass of bright-colored flames. It lit the desert and for an instant I could see hundreds of the coyotes bursting into flame all around us before everything went black. The light immolated them to one. One minute they were there, the next they were crumpled balls of flame, then the world was dark and quiet.

"It is okay Christopher. You vision should return shortly."

Old Ying's soft voice.

"What happened? Girl! You okay?"

Wasco's gravely growl.

"She is fine, Mr. Wasco. I am here with her, although I cannot see at this moment either. Ying can, and we are all fine." Li's calm soft voice.

"What was that? What happened?" My voice and my body were shaking. I couldn't find my gun, must have dropped it somewhere. I started to scramble trying to find it. Ying's soothing voice and firm grip kept me still.

There was warmth on my leg; either blood or I had finally pissed myself. I wanted to stand up but was afraid to.

"Ying, what the hell did you do?" Wasco asked from somewhere off to my left.

"I summoned spirits of the sun. The spirits of the sun hate the creatures of darkness, so they destroyed them. Unfortunately, they also burn so brightly they can blind." Ying said. "Mr. Wasco, you have been bitten at least a few times. I need to tend to those wounds immediately."

"Naw, I'm alright Ying. Check on the others first. Bites ain't that deep and the Black Rot won't hurt me."

"Ms. Ying, I am afraid that Jacob is not here." Li's voice again. "I saw him earlier. He was, uh, being dragged away."

"What? Where is he?" I asked. My stomach was sick, and I thought I might puke."

"I believe he is fine Christopher, he is just over the ridge. I saw him go as well. Li will go and collect him in a moment," she said.

When the last spots finally left, and I was able to see again, I might as well still have been blind. The fire was completely gone, and the night was pitch black. Only the stars told me that my sight had returned. Li began another small fire and Ying cleansed any wounds that were rotted. Once she was satisfied with Li's wounds she sent him to retrieve Jacob and worked on mine. Wasco was covered in blood. Some his, some the coyotes. When the fire illuminated him, I swear the blood was moving, flowing around the bite marks, and following the little burn scars on his body that now looked like intricate designs. It was mesmerizing, and I stared until Wasco turned his head and said Li was coming back. I looked where he was but couldn't see anything in the darkness.

Soon I made out movement and my hands tightened on the Winchester. He was alone.

When he stepped into the firelight he said, "I found where he was. A lot of coyote bodies and much blood. In the sand there is an imprint where he fell, but he is not there."

He was covered in sweat and breathing hard, his chest heaving air in controlled deep breaths.

"How far?" Wasco asked.

"Near half a mile I would guess," he replied.

"Show me," Wasco said and got up. I stood as well but he put his hand up. "Need to find tracks, the fewer people stompin' around the easier it'll be. Stay here."

I started to protest, caught myself and bit my lip until it bled. They walked off and I just stared after them. I might have dozed off, maybe I didn't, everything was confusing, and my mind was having trouble focusing.

"Someone took him," Wasco said when he came back into camp.

"Ain't gonna be able to track them in the dark and we're too beat up. Nothin' to do but get some rest and be ready at first light."

I was too stunned to say anything. Ying frowned, then nodded and walked to her bedroll by the fire. Li followed, and Wasco set to packing everything we didn't immediately need. I'm not sure what happened, at some point I sat down and then I woke up sore and cold in the dirt with Ying gently shaking me. The sun was up but no direct sunlight was hitting us yet because of the cliff to the east. I shivered in the morning air and numbly gathered my things. Someone, probably Wasco, had put a blanket over me in the night, and I kept that wrapped tight around me.

By the time I was on Old Shit's back I had remembered what had happened and I was shaking from more than the cold. We rode in silence with Wasco leading his horse as he followed the tracks. I tried not to look at the still-smoking bodies of the coyotes as we rode, but I could not avoid the stench. The most disturbing thing was I was so hungry, and it smelled like cooked meat, which made my mouth water until I remembered what it was, then I would dry heave.

After a couple of hours, Wasco stopped us and passed out some hard bread. By then I was awake, and I was getting angry at not knowing what was going on, combined with not wanting to ask. I was afraid someone might tell me the answer.

"Well," Wasco said pointing to the sheer cliff face ahead. "I'm pretty sure Jacob is alive. The drag marks stopped awhile back and a new set of barefoot tracks started. They lead to them rocks there. "

I hadn't been paying much attention so I was surprised to find that we had been riding straight toward the cliff. Edge City and the mines stared down as if in judgment. The ground was littered with giant piles of rocks and pieces of metal apparently tossed from the mines. Scattered across the base of the cliff were caves and crevasses where any number of creatures could be living. I pulled out my spyglass and scanned the side of the wall. With a start I dropped the glass and gasped.

"What is it girl?" Wasco asked.

"I saw something," I said and pointed. "It was looking right back at me!"

Wasco bent and handed me back the spyglass.

"Well, ain't no sense tryin' to sneak up then. Let's go see if they got Jacob," he said, grabbed the reins of his horse, and started walking. The rest of us climbed off our mounts and followed. Li gave a quick count of the arrows he had managed to recover from the coyote fight that were now in his quiver and then set one to his bow. After a few more steps I pulled the Winchester from its holster and cocked it. The noise echoed around the rocks. Wasco looked back and gave me a nod. I had been expecting a glare.

We walked into the sandy, rock-strewn field, everyone on edge and looking around. When we were close enough to see the cave I had spotted, there was nothing there. Wasco headed toward an old dead tree and loosely wrapped the reins of his horse around it, we all did the same. Then he set about looking at the ground.

"Might as well start where ya seen something girl, too rocky to see where they went," he said.

We walked between two huge fallen rocks and into the darkness. The passage made a slow curve, so the sunlight was quickly gone. It felt like we were going down, but I wasn't sure. Ying took out a small vial, popped the cork and whispered something into it. She then replaced the cork and the vial began to glow softly. It was not bright, but in the blackness of the tunnel it was enough. We walked slowly, everyone on edge. Except Wasco; he was on guard. At an intersection he bent to look at something on the floor and pointed to the left with his rifle. We followed.

After a while, the tunnel leveled out and opened to a large cavern. I am not sure how I knew that. I think I could just feel the openness. Without the close sides of the passage for the light to reflect from, it seemed as if the darkness consumed the meager light from Ying's vial.

Wasco stopped. I bumped into him and Ying into me. I had no idea where Li was.

A sound echoed around the cavern. *Psst, click, clank*. We froze, listening for more sounds and looking for movement in the inky black of the cave. Then again, something mechanical. It repeated with a regular cadence that was quite ominous, getting louder, getting closer.

Psst, click, clank. Then there was a pinpoint of light, a spark. Then a fire blazed to life some yards ahead of us. The suddenness of it blinded me at first, but as my vision cleared and adjusted, a figure took shape, silhouetted by the fire he held. At first, he was just a blob, hulking, but vaguely human, coming toward us. As he got closer I was able to make some details though I wished I hadn't. *Psst, click, clank.* The clank ringing out each time his right foot hit the stone.

Wasco called out for him to stop where he was and raised his rifle. He did. Nobody moved. Nobody spoke. Hours passed in those seconds while everyone waited.

Then, *sssst, click, pffft*, and it spoke.

"Why are you here?"

It sounded like a growl made into words.

"Ya took one of ours," Wasco called. "Aim to get him back."

The thing was silent for a while, and then raised an arm.

I heard grunts, clanking, and whirring, then footsteps coming from the darkness behind him.

A few paces before they were even with him, the first one started forward with the rest fanning out behind him. Wasco adjusted his grip on the rifle. I tried cocking the Winchester and realized it was already done then looked around to see if anyone had noticed.

Some of them were carrying hammers, picks, and clubs. Others had them on broad backs or hanging from belts. A few were wearing guns at their hips or carrying rifles.

They were not human. They were a combination of green humanoid and pieces of metal machinery. The sound they made as they came was not as loud as you might think; it was an almost melodic combination of clicks, dings, whirrs, and gongs. Some of them moved with a lithe grace that surprised me, while others plodded along with heavy footfalls. There was something odd about the way they moved. Like they had been broken into pieces, put back together, and were relearning how to move.

The leader stopped about ten feet from Wasco and the others fanned out to his sides—about six of them I think. He had a square jaw and his shoulders were broad but seemed to have some kind of metal armor on them so it was hard to tell what was him and what might have been armor or machine. He was tall but stood hunched over, so he looked much shorter than I think he really was. His eyes were a contrast to the heavy brow and harsh lines of the rest of his face. They were alive with life and twinkled brown in the torchlight, and he had wrinkles at the corners, like someone who smiled a lot. As he breathed I noticed steam streaming from his wide nostrils and between two large tusks that protruded from his lower jaw.

His head would twitch every few seconds accompanied by a metallic clicking sound. There was a hinged iron lever coming out of his neck that jumped when that happened.

His right arm was covered in the clean, white, cotton sleeve of his shirt, but his left had the sleeve cut off at the bicep. Out of the sleeve a muscled green bicep ended in a metal pivot that anchored what looked like a cannon. One foot was also a clump of metal. As I looked closer it actually looked like a steel pick instead of a foot, like something miners carried.

He noticed my stare and turned his head with a whirr and a click and smiled at me. His eyes crinkled just like I had expected they would. Even with those tusks, the smile turned him from monster to pleasant man in an instant. It was one of those smiles that you just know is genuine. I smiled back.

"*Sssst, click, pffft*. My name is Samrak," he said.

"I'm Topher," I said. "This is Wasco, Ying, and..."

I realized only then that Li was nowhere to be found. Ying's eyes met mine and held them a moment.

"Wasco and Ying from Edge City," I said.

"*Sssst, click, pffft*. Come, let us sit and we will tell you of your friend. We meant him no ill will and caused him no harm." He turned, as did most of those with him in a cacophony of metallic clicks, pings and clangs accompanied by puffs of air and steam.

A few didn't immediately turn to go. They stood tense and a few hands had found the handles of weapons. Wasco didn't move. He had locked gazes with one of the threatening green men and the two looked ready to charge each other at any minute. Samrak turned back and saw the standoff. He stormed around the offender, cutting its stare from Wasco's and locked his own with it. Words passed between them, but I could only hear what sounded like growls. A few tense seconds passed, and the challenger turned and stalked off, his apparent followers falling in behind him.

Samrak stalked after them without a glance back to us. After a moment of hesitation Wasco looked to us, shrugged, and we followed them into the gloom of the cave.

I watched the things that walked in front of us. Almost all were misshapen in some way, even under the metallic bits and various shades of green. There was something about some of the misshapen bodies that rang familiar to me, but I was unable to place it.

As we came into their camp I saw Jacob. He was sitting against a wall, his head cocked to the side. His eyes didn't focus on us, didn't even blink.

"Jacob!" I cried and ran towards him. One of the creatures started to reach out to me, but a wave and a look from Samrak stopped them.

Jacob did not move. Didn't acknowledge me. I spun on them.

"What did you do to him?" I screamed.

I would have started shooting right then had I not dropped my Winchester when I ran to him.

"*Ssssst, click, pffft*. He has been drugged," Samrak said.

A growl crept through the cavern. Everyone looked around at first, thinking it an animal or the rock walls themselves. It had come from Wasco. All eyes eventually focused on him and nobody moved. He looked like he was about to kill everyone in that room.

"I dunno what or who you are, but you better consider yer next words carefully," Wasco said. His eyes burned holes in Samrak and I swear he grew ten feet!

Samrak seemed to grow as well and I thought I heard a growl from him. The two faced each other for a long time before he said, "*Ssssst, click, pffft*. We did him no harm; the drug is meant to ease pain, although there is more. If you want to listen, then I will explain."

Steam leaked from between his tusks every few words and there was an implied, *Or else.*

Wasco's hands tightened on his rifle. More seconds passed so slow I swear my hair grew.

Ying stepped up and said, "That will be fine, Mr. Samrak. All who came into this cave with us accept your offer of hospitality and will honor it and listen to what you have to say."

Samrak's gaze flicked to Ying and held there for a few long seconds. He cocked his head to the side then nodded and turned away, indicating we should follow. I felt, without really understanding, a quiet rumbling of discontent that spread through those watching from shadows at Ying's words and Samrak's agreement.

I had never been down into the mines, but the metal and machines I saw as I looked around are what I thought I would have seen if I had. Among the piles of metal and machines was an area filled with canvass and hide tents, a small kitchen area, and heavy wooden tables that had been reinforced in some spots with metal. Samrak led us to one of the long tables.

"*Sssst, click, pffft*. Sit," Samrak said.

Wasco pulled a chair from a table and sat. "Okay, talk. Who are you? What are you? And what the hell did you do to Jacob and why?"

Samrak sat down as did two others from his group. One was about Wasco's size, but older, with a grey beard flowing from below his yellowed tusks. He had very little in the way of metal or machinery attached to him. The other was a woman, not large, but muscled and lithe. She reminded me of a hunting cat. She was disfigured in a way that's hard to describe. It was as though her upper body wasn't put onto the lower half quite right. She also had tusks every bit the size of the others. She had black hair that hung to her shoulder on one half of her head, the other side was bald and smooth as if it had never had hair. Her pale skin stood in contrast to her deformed figure, being a smooth, even pretty, shade of light green.

"*Sssst, click, pffft.* Some of those are things that may not be any of your business," Samrak said. "I will start with the last."

"Your friend was found in the sands by some of our scouts that we send to gather, um, scrap. They found him and gave him a tonic to ease his pain and keep him slumbered."

"Why?" growled Wasco.

"That gets us into the rest of your questions," Samrak said.

He paused while a woman set some metal cups and a bottle on the table. She was young looking, but when she turned to go I caught sight of the other side of her. She was missing half the skin on her face and on her left hand. There was just bone. It looked like it had been sealed with some strips of metal that were screwed into the bones. Hoses ran to various places on her and each finger had three small wires going to them. I couldn't help my stare. I just couldn't look away.

After the requisite clinking and clacking, Samrak said, "Elsa there is a good example of what I am going to tell you." He glanced at the woman's retreating form. "But first I must have your word that you do not speak of any of this when you leave. We do not normally let others see us. If people knew who and what we are, it would hurt all involved."

"Why?" Wasco said.

"*Sssst, click, pffft.* Because," Samrak said. "We are dead. Or at least we are to any that knew us. And the people who we left behind cannot know we still live. It will hurt them in most cases, and in some endanger our lives and theirs."

Wasco eyed him for a few silent seconds then said, "Go on."

"*Sssst, click, pffft*. Did you notice Elsa's appearance? My own rugged handsome qualities?"

He held up what I thought was his good hand and I noticed something I had missed before. It was on wrong! His whole arm was just wrong, twisted in an angle that made the hand face backwards when it ought to face forward.

"What happened?" I asked.

Samrak looked to me and smiled again. I am sure the ridiculousness of my asking about one injury to his arm given most of him was green, just as mangled and part metal was not lost on him. But I was young.

"*Sssst, click, pffft*. When I hit the ground, my arm was shattered, and my neck broken."

"Hit the ground?" I asked.

"I was a miner many years ago. I do not even remember how long it has been. Many down here are miners; others had been broken by the steam in the city. I was mining silver when the first veins of Ember were found. Nobody had figured out exactly how to get it out of the rock yet, or what in the hell it really was. It was in a shaft off the Edge wall, just a few hundred feet in.

Sssst, click, pffft. One day the boss sent me and my crew down to see if we could dig some out. None of us took it too seriously, just figured it was some worthless rock. We worked just inside of the shaft, so we still had sunlight close by and we didn't need to get lanterns and such. That's how we figured out that it turned color in the sunlight. Went from black to deep translucent green when we carried it into the sun to have a closer look. After a few hours of work, we managed to get a few ounces of the stuff. We had just carried the last bit out into the sun when we saw the storm clouds blowing in.

"We ran back in to grab our tools and Bill stuffed the Ember into his pockets. We hadn't made it far when the rain started, a downpour like I had never seen. First rain we'd had in a long time too. It soaked us pretty good, so we headed back into the shaft. None of us wanted to try to make the climb in that downpour, figured we'd wait it out.

"*Sssst, click, pffft.* That's when we learned the other thing about Ember. It turns water to steam. Bill jumped up and started slapping at his pockets, steam billowing out of his clothes. He panicked I guess, took off running into the mineshaft. We took off after him but lost him. Didn't have lanterns or even torches and the mines, they're like a maze. We had to go slow or risk falling into a down shaft or pool. Like Bill had.

"We heard his screams first, then the splashing. We ran as fast as we dared in the pitch black, but it wasn't fast enough. Bill had fallen into one of the underground lakes. It was just a small pool, not even very deep from the look of it. My pick-man Sinclair jumped in after him to try and help. There was so much steam, too much commotion, too much screaming.

"At first I just stood there. I didn't know what to do. They were fighting on the water; Sinclair was trying to haul Bill out. I think Bill's skin was being boiled from his bones and he didn't know what he was doing. I'd worked with Bill for years. He was always levelheaded, calculating even. I never would have imagined he could act like that, so he must have been in some terrible pain. The rain swollen tunnels must have reached their capacity. Water crashed down the shaft in a torrent, carrying even more of the steaming rock. Bits from here and there that had been left unnoticed during normal mining I guess. It all gathered into that one little pool. The force of it washed me from my feet, the steam burning my skin and eyes as I slid toward the boiling pool.

"My hand caught a hold of a rock and I clung there as the water rushed by. Then it stopped. It seemed so sudden. There was no sound of struggle, just dripping water echoing through the mines. I called out to them both, but nobody answered. Then I heard Bill laugh. It started like a giggle but then turned into a full-blown gut laugh."

Samrak looked off into the darkness like he was seeing something, or maybe hearing something. He looked sad.

"*Sssst, click, pffft*. I think I meant to run for help, that's what I try to tell myself. Maybe I was just afraid. I don't know. I wonder every night.

"I got to the shaft mouth and stopped, looking up at the path still awash with running water and sludge. I was afraid I would be swept off if I tried for the top. Indecision held me as sure as fear did. I think I had decided to go back for them because I had just started to turn when someone pushed me. Sinclair maybe? Bill? I don't know, but I was falling. Spinning in the air trying to find something to grab, anything to save me. All I found was death. The only thing I saw was Death's own face grinning at me as I tumbled off the edge.

"*Sssst, click, pffft*. I woke up surrounded by piles of old mining equipment, my leg pinned under a piece of steal. Companies had been tossing old drilling rigs and equipment over for years and I landed on it. Some of it had landed on me.

"My arm was shattered, and my head just flopped around. My neck was clearly broken, but somehow, I was alive. I later learned I had been there for weeks at least, maybe months, I am really not sure. Anyhow, She was there. I didn't know Her yet, but She had been nourishing me, keeping my body alive."

He looked up as if surprised we all looked puzzled.

"Mother," he said as if that explained everything. Maybe it had to Ying, because she nodded her head slightly.

"At first it was just the vines," he continued. "They were growing over and through all of the debris and me as well.

"It took me a long time to realize that some of them had grown into my skin. Burrowed into my organs and were pumping some kind of paste right into my guts and air into my lungs. Not understanding what was going on, I pulled at them and tried to stand, but my muscles wouldn't work. The vines must have known I was trying to move. *She* must have known. The vines wrapped me up and lifted my broken body.

"At first, I was mesmerized. I thought that I must have been hallucinating. Then I felt the pain. It was incredible. A wave of the worst pain I had ever felt crashed over me and then I was falling again. When I next woke up I was in the dark. My neck had been fused with bits of metal. Other bits held my leg together and my arm was gone. The pain was still there but I was able to bear it. I stayed there, in that cave for many months, vines feeding directly into my gut, helping me heal, teaching me to move, changing me.

"After months of recovery under the not-so-tender care of the plants and vines, I was able to feed myself. My body got strong, stronger than it had ever been. I went hunting, fishing, and eventually learned I was not alone in having been kept alive by Mother. Robinarl here found me, and we found others. We still didn't know Her. It was just the vines, but they nursed and brought back those we found that could be saved.

"*Sssst, click, pffft.* That was many years ago. Since then miners have fallen, people have jumped. Soon we learned of Her presence and that the vines were Her loving arms. Each time someone falls, Mother pieces them back together with bits of machinery. Using the metal castaways from the mines to repair the castaways of flesh. Bringing us all back into Her embrace. Over the years we have learned how to guide the process some. But it still doesn't happen easy and it hurts in ways you cannot imagine.

Mother does not tolerate those too weak to survive her love, but she did give us the resources to ease it some, to grow our numbers. One day Doc Parson fell to us. When he left Her embrace he said that She had told him a way to make the change easier so that more would survive. He created a drug to ease the pain of the transformation. It makes them more accepting of the change in body and mind. Many who were first brought from Her care were unable to cope with all they had endured. Many died before She granted us that boon.

We send regular patrols looking for any who have fallen. We give them the drug right away if they are alive. Then the Mother puts them back together. That is why we took your friend. One of our patrols found him and thought him a Fallen, so they gave him the elixir and brought him here.

"*Sssst, click, pffft*. It was not until you showed up that we realized the mistake."

"That is a hell of a tale yer tellin," Wasco said. "Can't imagine you making it up, so where does that leave us? He gonna be alright?"

"He will be better in a matter of hours without another dose. The amount we use at first is small," Samrak said.

"Is he gonna turn green like you?" I asked.

Wasco tensed, Ying sat up straighter, but Samrak just laughed. It looked weird coming from that tusked mouth with steam puffing out in little clouds. The others laughed too, and soon Wasco and Ying also chuckled.

I didn't see what was so damn funny.

"No little one, he won't. That is a result of whatever Mother does to us. Something She feeds us, so our bodies can accept the metal, Doc thinks. Unless we give him to Her, he will retain his pink skin."

"What the hell is this damn Mother you keep on about? You named the flowers that done this to ya?" Wasco asked.

After I had asked about being green, I thought I might have said something wrong, but everyone laughed. Wasco's question, they didn't laugh at.

Everything happened fast. Samrak jumped to his feet, I thought it was to attack Wasco, but I think it was to stop the other guy that came at a full charge hitting Wasco with a thunderous blow meant to take his head off. Wasco having reacted to Samrak standing took the blow on the meat of his shoulder instead, but it still knocked him back and over the table.

The woman turned to grab at me, so I jumped under the table and crawled to the other end. The old-looking guy yelled something in protest and reached for a knife at his belt as he turned on Ying who was on her feet but didn't seem to be watching him. I saw the hand pull the knife from the sheath from my spot under the table, tried to yell but there was too much commotion to be heard. Samrak was yelling for everyone to stop, but nobody seemed to be listening.

I had left the Winchester where I had been sitting so I crawled back to get it after seeing the woman move away. I popped my head up and an arrow appeared in the table next to it. Well, not the table precisely, it had first gone clean through the old guy's hand. The knife clattered to the floor.

Li dropped lightly onto the table from the darkness above, kicking out with his leg and knocking the old guy clean out before somersaulting off the table and over Samrak, catching him around the neck with his bow as he did. The momentum of his flip carried Samrak back and slammed him to the ground. Li had an arrow out and drawn in a blink, pointing right at Samrak's chest.

Wasco meanwhile had rolled to his feet and was trading heavy punches with the guy that had challenged him when we had arrived. The girl was now on the other end of the table, where I had been crawling to before I turned back for my gun, which I then pointed at her as I stood up.

Ying's voice echoed through the cavern, stopping everyone with its intensity. She was holding one of her vials near her mouth. There was a ripple of air over it, like the air above the hot sand.

"You have broken the Tenet of Hospitality. Cease or be destroyed."

I had no idea what she was talking about, but it worked. Everyone stopped. Well almost. The guy fighting Wasco took that moment to pull a pistol from the strap at his belt and point it at Wasco, who like everyone, had turned at the echoing boom of Ying's command.

The gun hit the rock, the draw having been interrupted by the arrow that had grown from his eye. Red and gold feathers quivered in the silence that followed before the body remembered it was dead and crumpled to the ground.

"Holy shit," I said.

Samrak got to his feet as Li stepped back and they locked eyes. Samrak looked like a storm trying to contain a twister. His eyes were hard, his muscles were tight, and steam was a constant angry hiss from his nostrils.

At first nobody moved. Besides the occasional click and clang of the green things, the cave was quiet.

Ying turned to Samrak and said, "We are here under the Tenet of Hospitality to which your leader agreed, and the Mother understands. It was broken through no action of ours. The life lost is your responsibility, not our own."

"You insulted her!" the woman I was pointing the Winchester at yelled.

"No. We did not. It was simply a misunderstanding of vernacular," Ying said.

"A what?" I asked.

"It is the way Mr. Wasco talks," Ying said. "A misunderstanding of the way he speaks and one that was easily clarified had he not been attacked." She looked at Samrak. "Do you disagree?"

Samrak was silent for a while then said, "I do not, but I will go to Mother and ask. If she does not honor your words, then you will not leave here."

He turned to the rest of the monster men and told them to leave. That's when I saw a side of Samrak that I had not known existed.

Some of his people refused to let it go. One stepped up to Samrak and snarled. Samrak laid him out with one blow to the side of his head. Another said something I could not hear and Samrak charged him and slammed him into the rock wall and growled. His face was so close to the others that the steam from Samrak's mouth actually went up the nose of the other one.

Seconds passed before the other one looked away and Samrak let him go and turned his back to him. No one else said anything.

He turned to Li and said, "This one was not a part of our Hospitality, he dies."

Two hulking green things stepped up to grab Li.

I screamed, "Samrak no!"

I was a kid; it was all I could think of.

Ying on the other hand, said in her calm quiet voice, "You are incorrect Samrak. I accepted your offer on behalf of all who entered this cave with us. This is Li; he is my servant and entered with us. It is not our fault that you failed to see him."

Samrak growled. "You play games with words little woman!"

"Do I?" she said with a pleasant smile on her wrinkled face. "And did I win this game of words?"

Samrak huffed a cloud of steam, turned, and walked away.

"Bring them," he said.

A gang of green muscle and metal bits surrounded us, and we were herded off into the darkness. I looked back to where

Jacob was. He was still sitting in the same place, eyes staring into the darkness. Wasco hesitated and looked as if he might try and take on the lot of them, but a touch on his arm and smile from Ying and he handed over his rifle. He did not look happy about it as he stalked after Samrak. Li handed over his bow and sword and a large green hand took my Winchester from me.

We followed Samrak into the darkness. As the light from the camp faded I noticed a green light in front of us. A pinpoint at first, that grew into a rectangle as we got closer. When we stopped, Samrak was waiting at a large metal door. The green light was leaking from the seams. He had lost the hard look, but his eyes didn't smile like they had before.

"*Sssst, click, pffft.* I will go and speak with Her. Watch them closely," he said to our guards. "If Mother tells me that they are false, they will be killed immediately. If they are true, She will tell me what to do next."

He looked at Wasco who had tensed and looked as if he was ready to throw himself at Samrak. Ying stepped in front of Wasco with another light touch to his arm.

"We will abide the judgment of your Mother," she said.

"The hell we wuuuurrrgh…" Wasco started to say before his voice just kind of stopped.

He looked perplexed then spun on Li who had reached up and tapped the side of Wasco's throat with one finger twice. Wasco tried again to say something, but no sound came out.

Ying said, "Yes, Mr. Wasco. We will. When something needs to be shot or beaten to a pulp, we will defer to you, but in this, you must defer to me. Your voice will return in a moment, now be still please."

Samrak stared hard at Ying for long seconds then turned and pulled hard on the heavy iron door which gave way with a creak.

The door was only opened for a moment, but it was enough. Green light flooded the cave, but it was not as intense as I think I had imagined it. Or maybe it just seemed brighter in the deep darkness of the cave. It was a soft, smooth, comforting light. It made me want to go to it. I think I actually took a step towards it, but Ying stepped in front of me which broke the trance. Just before the door closed I saw a room filled with vines that looked a lot like the Drinker root we used for our spitshots, except they were bright green. They were pulsating like Drinker roots too, pumping something into giant leafy pods. The last image I had is the silhouette of a twisted human figure inside one of those pods while one of the pulsating vines moved a large metal hinge into it, where the leaves then continued the pulsing push.

It should have been horrifying. I should have had nightmares about it, but it wasn't – and I didn't.

I didn't think anyone said or did anything while Samrak was gone. But I couldn't say for sure. I just remember the door opening and him coming out.

"The Mother says they are not false; they are to be allowed to go free," he said, then looked at one of the guards. "Go and get the other one and their weapons. I want them out of this cave immediately."

"What about Jacob," I said. "Will he wake up?"

"He will wake up, young Topher," Samrak said.

No one said anything until the guard retuned with Jacob walking numbly along with him. All our weapons and belongings that had been taken were pooled in his arms as he walked. I ran over to him and started taking everyone's belongings from him after giving the guard a dirty look and sticking my tongue out when he turned his back on me.

The others came and got theirs as well.

Samrak said, "Go," as he and his guards turned and walked away.

CHAPTER EIGHT – SNAKEFACE

We made good time getting away from the caves, mostly riding in silence. Wasco led us to a stream that was running from the mountains rather than the runoff from the mine. Since we were close to the cliffside it hadn't gone far enough to be contaminated by whatever turned everything black in that place.

"Don't drink it," Wasco had told us." It's safe to wash up in but keep it outta yer mouth."

I spent some time cleaning my clothes and washed up a bit as did the others. Each of us got some time while the others sat with their backs turned. My pants had been splattered with blood from the fight with the coyotes, and probably some urine if I'm honest. I washed them and set them out to dry then put on my other pair. We ate and mostly sat in silence until we were ready to move again. Jacob woke and seemed fine, not even a scratch really, but he was quiet, and we let him be.

"How we gonna sleep out here again? I ain't seen no rocks anywhere," I asked.

The thought of another night in the open turned my guts to water.

"Should be alright," Wasco pointed out into the distance. "Over there it starts getting hilly. Looks like dunes from here but it ain't. Rocks and hills. There should be Movers in there too. Only a few hours from here, let's get a move on."

He was right. Within a couple of hours, I realized we were going up when my back started aching from leaning forward. An hour after that and it was rocky ground. Black and sharp hard rock, but it did seem a little less imposing nonetheless.

We stopped early in a semi-circle of rocks and Movers, and Wasco had a fire going in minutes. We cooked stew and even softened some of the hard bread in the coals. Overall, it was comfortable. You wouldn't know we were in the middle of the Blacklands and had almost been eaten by black-toothed, goo-drooling coyotes, or turned into green monsters by whatever those other things were. I kept hoping one of the Movers would snuggle near me like the one had done, but none did. They would shuffle a little here and there, but that was all.

"Ying, what did you mean in Samrak's cave about Tenets of Hospitality? Why'd that make everyone stop fighting?" I asked through a mouthful of bread.

She set her bowl down, wiped her mouth and said, "You have seen the things I do when I talk to spirits. They have rules Topher. The thing that Samrak and his clan called The Mother was a spirit. I felt it as soon as we entered the cave. I could not talk to it as I do the elemental spirits, but I could hear it talking to them. Somehow that spirit has found a way to connect itself to Samrak's people. It is a spirit of nature, of plants I believe, but there is something more. It is angry. Filled with a rage that is hardly contained. I cannot begin to tell you the source of its anger, but it was there."

"I felt it too," I said.

She smiled. "I am sure you did." For some reason I didn't understand she looked at Wasco when she said it and I almost think he nodded.

"Anyway, when dealing with spirits, even those corrupted as I believe The Mother to be, one must know the rules. I do, as did Samrak in a very primitive way. Tenets are the guiding rules that insure the spirits of the world do not destroy each other in constant battle. Certain behaviors are expected, and if they are not adhered to other spirits will shun the offender. Since spirits cannot always avoid each other, those rules are for self-preservation, and possibly the preservation of the world."

Wasco rumbled his agreement or something and stood up. "I'll be back in a bit, gonna scout the trail ahead to see if I can find any sign of them bandits. Topher, mind if I borrow that spyglass?"

I stood up, pulled it from my belt and walked it over to him. He must have seen the question in my eyes. He rested a heavy hand on my shoulder.

"I know ya want to come, but ya can't. You're learnin' to move quiet and even shoot pretty good, but not good enough for out here, not for this."

"All right," I said trying to sound casual. "Just seein' if ya needed help is all."

He looked over me to the others. "Keep things quiet and the fire low, we might be closer than we think." Back to me he said, "And no shootin' the Movers."

He went on foot, moving with a grace that always seemed wrong on a man that size, although his limp was worse, and he kept swinging his left arm around, and holding the shoulder. I watched him till he was out of sight then sat back down and found I didn't know what to do with myself.

I was exhausted but couldn't sleep. I pushed the ashes of the fire around a little, straightened my bedroll again, dug in my pack for some candy, found I was out, and cussed. The others weren't saying much either. Not for any reason, things were pleasant enough considering, there was just nothing to say or do. I took out my spitshot and fired a couple of chips into a cactus, but it was getting slow and there wasn't any Drinker root around, so I stopped.

I went over and sat next to Jacob. He flinched but didn't move away. He hadn't been himself since he woke up from the drugs, but I didn't think much of it.

"So, how'd you learn to shoot so good?" I asked.

"It, well it just came naturally, really. Kinda like you and that spit thing. I was good at it and I got in enough trouble to have to do it a lot."

He smiled. The smile I had been waiting for.

"Why do you think Wasco fought for the Union instead of the Empire? My pa said the Union were all traitors to the Empire and the Empire is the way things oughta be."

"Your father said that? Was he African too?" he asked.

"Of course he was chucklehead!" I said.

"I, well that is, um. Well the Empire, they view Africans as, well..."

"Yeah, I know, he told me, we weren't as good as the white skins. The Enlightened say we were meant to serve white people. Ma says that's bullcrap. Sounds like bullcrap to me, too. I don't serve nobody nothin'!" I declared.

Jacob smiled. "Yes, it is bullcrap, Topher, and don't you forget it. The Union are not traitors to them either. The

Terralibre nation is the people that stayed here through the Curse. They had been here so long the Native's Curse didn't affect them as much, so they could still grow some food is what I heard. When the Enlightened Empire came trying to take over, they fought them with the Africans and the Natives trying to hold them back."

"Ma said that our people helped make the Curse too," I said.

"That is what they say. I know that many of your people were slaves when the settlers first came over, and that the Curse helped free them. Nobody seems to know how exactly, just that it did. You know that your people are part of the Nations, don't you? You have a country," he said.

"I know. No matter to me. I'm happy here with all you white people. Makes my skin look even better!" I rubbed my dark arms. I was so proud of my black skin. "Glad I ain't no slave though."

We were quiet for a while, and then I asked, "Were you in the war?"

"No. My pap was, sort of. He didn't fight for either side, but for a few years, everybody was in the war one way or the other," Jacob said.

"What is the Enlightenment anyway?" I asked. "I mean, I know what my ma and pa said, and what the other kids say, and there are some of them in the Ends that preach about it and give me dirty looks, but why do they think they are better than everyone else? What do they want that I should do about being African?"

Jacob took a breath and let it out slowly.

"Did you go to school, Topher?" he asked.

"Na. Kids in the Ends don't go to school," I said.

"Ah," he said. "Well, let's see. The Enlightened came over after the Curse had ended. Those that had been run off by the Curse and still held to thinking this was their land. When they got back to Europe, that's across the sea where they are from, there was a thing called Enlightenment. It was popular in Europe around then. They didn't have bad ideas really, not all of them at least, but some of them were convinced only they were smart enough to be in charge.

"They had some crazy ideas. The folks that fled back to Europe from here when the Curse hit joined that group of crazies and started planning to come back here and start an Empire based on those crazy ideas. When word arrived that the land here was producing again and the Curse was over, they put their plans into motion and left Europe, taking a bunch of the ships and armies of the counties they were from. Mostly England and Prussia I think. Those are countries across the ocean. In Europe.

When they arrived out east they declared themselves the Enlightened Empire and set about taking over. The Terralibre people had made a sort of peace with the Tribes and were coexisting with them and tried to fight the Enlightened. The Empire mostly whipped them and took over most of the north and east. They were stopped when they got to the southwest and the Natives, who knew something like this was going to happen, had been preparing.

"So, they joined with Terralibre to fight them. Called the army the Union. That was the war Wasco fought in. The last of the wars for the country that sort of settled things as they are now. You grew up in Edge City, which is the only place not claimed by either Natives, the Enlightened Empire, or Terralibre, all because of Ember."

I didn't say anything after that, just sat thinking deep thoughts.

Li and Ying sat across the fire and talked in their own language once in a while. The afternoon became evening and Wasco returned.

"Yeah, we're right on top of them alright," he said after taking a seat and handing me back my spyglass. "Just over the ridge there. A fort or somethin'. One of them airship things was takin' off, so I'd say it's our man. They got a big building that looked to be a chow…harrr oof glurgh…"

He crumpled over face first into the fire, showering the evening sky with sparks. Jacob was on his feet and firing his pistols that were again somehow in his hands.

On a rock the direction Wasco had come from was a monster that made my skin crawl. At first, I thought it was a Native, but its lower half was a giant snake. It held a short bow in its hand and was reaching for another arrow while it dodged the hail of bullets from Jacob's guns. I grabbed the Winchester and added my bullets to the air. They all missed. The snake-man-thing was too fast to get a bead on.

Li was on the move with his own bow, maneuvering around to flank the thing. Wasco hadn't moved, and the fire was roaring around his head. I desperately wanted to help him but couldn't stop shooting or that thing might have time to shoot back. It spun on Li and fired an arrow at him that careened off his armor. Li fired back and barely missed. That gave Jacob a chance to reload just as I heard the click of my own ammo running out.

The thing drew a bead on me and I froze. Everything froze. Jacob had just finished dropping the last bullet into his pistol and snapping the cylinder closed, but his other he had holstered after reloading.

"Drop gun," the thing slurred to him. "Or the boy dies."

Jacob dropped it. The thing looked at Li's bow and swung his head to indicate he should toss it. He did. Ying had been trying to pull Wasco from the fire.

"Leave him," came the command in broken English. "Now you come."

He indicated with his bow for Ying to move over by Li, and then he did the same to Jacob.

"I do not think I will," Jacob said.

The thing looked back at him. "I will kill the boy." His bow locked on me again and he drew back the arrow.

"Yeah, you said that, but I don't think you're fast enough."

Snakeface just stared at him.

"You gave me too much time see. I got your measure now. And, you did not think to address this fine Cooper double-action pistol sitting in my left holster. You are some kind of snake-man I see. Some people say I am too. So, I'm thinking I can draw this pistol out of my holster and shoot you before you can let loose of that arrow you got there. What do you say we give it a go?"

Nobody moved. All the snake thing had to do was open his fingers and I was dead. I heard a pop as Jacob flexed his finger. I jumped. The snake thing let loose his arrow; I heard a shot, then another. It happened so fast that they almost sounded like one shot. The arrow exploded about halfway to me, showering me with splinters but not hurting me. I opened my eyes and watched the snake man as it fell off the rock and landed with a thud. Li leapt on it and Ying ran to Wasco. I shook.

Then I turned to Jacob and yelled, "What the hell was that chucklehead? Ya coulda got me stuck through with an arrow! How the hell did you shoot an arrow?"

My fear let loose of me when I saw Wasco out of the corner of my eye, blood was frothing out of his back where Ying had removed the arrow. That wasn't good, I knew that. He was probably all burned up too. I ran over to him to see, but his head and face were fine. Like nothing had happened. Except for a small bone ring stuck in his ear that was glowing reddish orange. I reached out to touch it and yanked my hand back. It was hot to the touch! He groaned and turned his head.

"Damned poison." Then his eyes closed.

Ying smeared some of the sweet-smelling salve she had used before onto the wound then forced a vial of the nasty tasting stuff down his throat.

"The arrow hit his lung. Only time can properly heal a wound like that. If the lung collapses, then he will die. The poison will need an antidote. Did Mr. Wasco not say the Apache Natives used sand lizard oil to poison their arrows? That...thing, I think was once Apache. We need to find a sand lizard. Come with me Topher, I will need your quick hands."

She stood and walked out of the circle of rocks holding onto my arm to look for sand lizards. The sun was almost down, and the night chill was setting in fast. I had forgotten to grab my jacket and was shivering. The shadows made it hard to see details and we didn't see a single living thing for a long time. We had wandered out of the rocky hill and onto the dunes below.

"Perhaps they seek cover at night?" Old Ying offered.

I flipped over one of the scattered stones and fell backwards as something came flying out at me. A flying scorpion landed on the hat Wasco had bought for me. I ripped it off my head and threw it and the scorpion flew off into the night.

"I am so glad that didn't land in my hair!" I said.

Ying picked up my hat and held it out to me; I took it gingerly, inspecting every inch and tapping it a few times before putting it back on.

"I'm going to go and get a stick to flip the next one," I said then trudged back up the dune toward the camp where the kindling was stacked.

"Just lay 'em down right there will be fine. That's right, nice and slow."

The voice filtered out from our camp on the wind, barely audible. It was no one I knew.

"Shit," I said, then froze and listened.

"He dead?" Another voice I didn't recognize.

"No, but he is gravely injured," Li said.

"Well, pick him up; if he lives maybe the boss'll want him."

I heard Li grunt in effort then say thank you, presumably to Jacob.

"Shit, shit, shit." I ran down the hill.

CHAPTER NINE – BELLA

"What are we going to do Ying? Those, those things have got them! Are they gonna eat them?"

"No child, they are not animals, they have at least some humanity in them. Had they wanted them dead they would have killed them by now."

We were in the cover of the rocks looking with the spyglass as the last of the sunlight slowly faded. A group of six, men, I guess. I don't know how to describe them. Like Snakeface they were people but had animal parts too. There was another snake-man, a man top-half on a giant scorpion body. *Probably had wings, too,* I thought. The others were hard to make out in the fading light; at least one I think was just a man. I don't know why I thought that. Jacob and Li were walking next to Old Shit with Wasco thrown over his back bobbing along.

"We need to follow them. Quickly child, gather up what you can."

I ran over and picked up the Winchester. I had dropped it when I had run to check on Wasco after the fight. They must not have seen it.

I had not had time to reload and the bullets were in my bag on Old Shit with my damn coat. I didn't see any other weapons, but there were some rations lying around and the bedrolls were still there. I gathered up two bedrolls and an extra blanket for Old Ying and rolled the rations into them using some cord to make shoulder straps.

Shouldering the pack, I went back to Ying. She smiled and took my elbow.

"Do not worry child, we will find a way," she said.

It was a long and depressing walk. We were both exhausted from lack of sleep. For whatever reason, I wasn't worried about the creatures of the Blacklands attacking. Maybe because it didn't feel like we were alone. The things that took the others were not our friends, but they were at least out there.

The fort had a tall wooden picket fence but no gate. Inside was a long wooden building surrounded by close to twenty tents. I hadn't realized we had come back so close to the cliff face again, but on the other side of the city. I could see its lights a few miles away and hundreds of feet up.

The fort was at the foot of a small dam in Black River. Black River really wasn't a river. At least not a natural one. It was anywhere from a trickle to a fast river that formed from the runoff water they used in the mines to wash away rock and dirt. It was almost constant these days, with water pouring from numerous openings day and night. The water came out black and steaming as bits of Ember activated when they were washed over. Most were caught in massive nets, but enough got by to activate in the falls and cause the steam that constantly enveloped the Ends and Chinatown.

Why the water was so black even this far away nobody knew nor cared. Yet these yahoos had bothered to dam it up. Surely nobody was fool enough to drink it I thought.

Ying and I snuck around the camp as close as we dared. By now we had guessed that Wasco had been seen when he was scouting, so we were especially careful. There were fires inside the fort so with the spyglass I was able to see in. They took the others across the camp and then I lost sight of them.

"What do we do?" I asked.

"I think," Ying said, "that I have something that might help. But I can make only a small amount. Enough for perhaps a small girl?"

"What is it?"

"Come, let us get to those rocks and out of sight, and I will show you.

We moved over to a small bunch of rocks that had been stacked, probably when they built the dam, and Ying started setting out little packets and vials.

"This will call the spirits of the water to you. With all the steam in the air from the river, they should be enough to hide you for a time, so you can sneak in and find our friends," she said.

I looked at her like she was crazy, remembering the thing that had killed the man in the wagon fight and gulped. She looked up at me.

She said, "That spirit was of air and only acted the way I had asked of it. Most spirits are neither good nor evil; they simply are what they are. I asked that one to take the air from that man and it did so, not knowing why or what it would do to the man. It did so because I have for many years talked to the spirits and they know me."

She mixed some powders into a vial, put a cork into it then shook it. She then opened a small clay jug and dumped the vial into it, while stirring it with a small stick. Then she set it aside. Steam started gathering around the top of it, but it was not coming from inside the bottle, it was gathering from the air around it. She held a small vial in front of my eyes and I blinked. I had been mesmerized by the gathering steam being pulled into the jar.

"This one is for Mr. Wasco or anyone else that is hurt. If no one else is, tell them to give the whole thing to Mr. Wasco. If someone is, have them first take a sip then give him the remainder," she said. She held another out. "This one is in case something happens to you. If you are injured drink it."

I took the vials and stuck them into the pocket of my deerskin vest.

"This," she said as she held up the stuff she had made, "is not for drinking. We will rub this onto your skin and clothes. You should take off your shoes too and do your feet. This will call the water spirits in the air to you and mist will surround you."

I made a face of disgust.

"Do not fear the mist; it will be pure from the spirits of water, not the foul stuff of the river. But the stuff from the river will help conceal you as well, so stay in the mists as much as you can. With it on your feet it will muffle the sound of your walking, but you can still be heard if you speak or make too much noise, so be stealthy."

I grinned, that was getting into what I knew. Somewhere in my head something was screaming I was supposed to be terrified, but I was too excited to hear it. I started smearing the stuff on. Nothing happened. I waited and looked at her.

She said, "Go ahead child, they are coming. Quiet as a mouse; see if you can free everyone safely. If not, at least we will know more."

I started walking and noticed little mist whirlwinds spinning behind me. My vision was a tad bleary, like when you first wake up, but I could see well enough; and if I tried, I could see small figures in the mist that surrounded me. I smiled so big my mouth hurt!

By the time I was halfway to the camp I could tell the mist had engulfed me. It was tickling my skin and swirling around me. I tried to walk into the thickest parts of the fog and move as quiet as I could.

Eventually I had to leave the ground fog and cross a large open space to get to the gate. I crept as slowly as I could and took my time. No one cried an alarm as I slipped in, keeping my back against the wall.

I almost shrieked when I saw the first guard. It was that beast that had a giant scorpion body. It wasn't close, maybe twenty feet away, but it was the scariest thing I had ever seen. I moved on, shaking. It looked over at me and I froze, but it just kept moving its gaze past me. *Neat*, I thought through the fear.

I headed for the corral I had seen previously and ducked under the rail. I had noticed Wasco's Appaloosa earlier when I was using the spyglass, so I figured I might as well see if they left anything I could use. It was still saddled. I patted it on the nose.

"Hey boy, they leave anything in here?" I asked him and started digging into the saddlebags. They had taken almost everything. All I could find was a handful of those colorful rifle balls that the fire rifle used at the bottom of a saddlebag.

I checked the other horses and didn't find anything useful. I patted Old Shit on the way out then headed for the main building. The fog was thick around it so once I got near it I felt safer.

I stood still for a long time looking for guards and listening. I only saw the one I had passed before. I thought I could hear some voices inside, but I wasn't sure. I crept along the wall and peeked in the first window. There was no one inside. The room was very clean and colorful.

A large featherbed took up one wall and a small vanity with a glass mirror sat against another. On it was a pearl-handled hair brush, some colored powders, and a perfume bottle. A woman's room. I hadn't seen any women among the monsters.

The next window was an office and also unoccupied. There was a desk made from thick-hewn rough lumber, a metal fireplace, and an old rifle hanging over the door. The door was closed and located directly across from the window. I kept going until I reached a center door that was propped open.

There were definitely voices coming from inside. It wasn't the others, but I couldn't hear what they were saying. Risking a look around the door frame I couldn't see anyone. It was a hall that ended in a large room. I crawled on hands and knees past it as fast as I could. Goosebumps popped up on my arms and I got a chill down my neck. I was sure someone would call out an alarm any minute. All I could think was how stupid this was and I should have stayed home. There was nothing to do but go forward and I desperately wanted to find Wasco and Jacob, so I kept moving.

No one cried an alarm and the fog thinned out as I got closer to the end of the building. I almost let loose another scream. Bodies were piled up as high as my head; horses, cows, big bugs, snakes, all kinds of things. If I would have wanted to keep looking I could have seen if the arm I saw was as human as it looked, but I didn't. I crept closer without looking at the pile, found the door I thought my friends had been taken in and cracked it open.

A long dark hallway stretched from one end of the building to the other. I gagged from the smell that hit me like a wall. I didn't see anything, so I slipped in and quietly pulled the door closed behind me. The mist still tickled my skin but seemed a little less. I moved slow as molasses, putting my feet down like Wasco had shown me. The floor was creaky as an old shoe, but I managed to avoid most of them. There was something humming down the hall that covered what noise I did make.

I had gone about halfway when I found cages. The walls were lined with them and I found the source of the stink. Whatever had been kept in those cages had not been let out to use a chamber pot. Hadn't even been given a chamber pot. Wasco and the others were in the last cell and it was no less filthy.

Jacob looked likely to have jumped right out of there when I said his name. I admit I might have chuckled a little.

"It's me, addle-brain. Now be quiet!" I scolded.

"Topher, what in tarnation are you doing here? You need to run!" Jacob said.

"Shh! You're too loud; there is a guard just over there. Now shut up! Here, is anybody hurt? Ying said if you're hurt to take a sip and give the rest to Wasco; if you ain't hurt then give it all to him." I held the vial through the bars.

Li came over and took it from me, went right to Wasco and poured it down his throat.

"He has not been well; I think his lung is collapsing."

"Ain't you hurt too? You're limping!"

"I will live without it," he said. "He would not. Where is Mistress Ying?"

"She's out there hidin'. How can we get out of here? Are there keys?"

I started looking around.

Jacob said, "Only in dime stories kid. They took them when they left like real people do."

"T... Topher."

Wasco. His voice was so small. I had never heard Wasco sound so weak.

"Yeah Wasco, I'm here. What is it?"

"Get Bella. I need Bella."

"Wha? I don't know what she looks like Wasco, and how's a horse gonna help?

"Not a damned horse, my rifle. I saw it when they drug me in here. It's in this building, hanging over a door," he said.

He could barely get the words out and he was breathing so hard!

"Yeah, I saw it I think," I told him.

"Wait what?" Jacob walked over to Wasco. "You mean to tell me Bella is a damn gun?" His voice was rising. "We come all this damn way, attacked Keaton enterprises, *for a damn gun*! I mean a horse, ok, maybe, I get it, but it's a damn gun!" He was almost shouting.

There was a heavy thud on the wall. "Shut yer damn mouth else I'll come in there and rip yer damn jaw off."

I froze. Jacob still looked incredulous. Li moved over and put his ear against the stained wall.

"Ain't just a damned gun, now get it fer me so we can get out of here," Wasco wheezed.

He seemed to be breathing a little easier, but not much. Jacob walked across the cell shaking his head and kicking straw.

"Yer getting paid, quit yer damn whinin'. Sound like a little girl," Wasco managed to say louder than was necessary.

"Quiet!" I near yelled, then covered my mouth and held my breath waiting for that thing to come crashing in. It didn't.

"I'm tellin' ya, it ain't just a damn gun, now hurry kid. I can't get any damn air. Git Bella, she'll help," Wasco said again.

I had no idea what to do. I figured he was delirious. I looked at Jacob and he shrugged.

"Maybe the keys are with it," I said. It was all I could think of. "I'll go check."

Jacob stared at me for a minute and then nodded and said, "Be careful kid. Those things, they are, they are not right."

"Nah! Really? I thought bein' half snake was stinkin' normal!" I said.

I padded back down the hall and peeked out the door. I didn't see the guard, so I poked my head out, then the rest of me, and scurried down to the window where I had seen the rifle. I realized in horror that tickle on my skin was gone at the same time I saw the guard. He was looking away from me at the moment, but his head was turning my way. Had that window been open or closed? I couldn't remember. It didn't matter.

I stood and leapt through the window waiting for the sound of breaking glass, arms over my face, which was a good thing, because I hit the floor face-first. No glass shattered, and my face only made a little cracking noise when my nose hit the floor. I was too scared to cry out or even whimper.

Tears were running down my face and my nose throbbed. I touched my nose and came away with blood and God did it hurt. It was bent at a weird angle and I almost puked. I couldn't do anything but lie there. I didn't even dare sniffle the blood that was running out and pooling on the floor.

What if that thing had seen me? Or heard me and was coming right now to grab me, and put me in one of those cages, or worse throw me on the pile after it…I couldn't complete the thought. I was panicking and shaking and about to cry, which with a broken nose would not have been quiet.

I thought about Jacob and Li in that gross cage, and Ying out in the Blacklands alone, and Wasco, barely able to breathe. Then I felt, I don't know what, something. A calmness that just fell over me like a blanket. It wrapped me up and all of a sudden I was no longer afraid. It took some time and many deep breaths, but I finally moved. Nothing grabbed me from the window and I didn't hear anyone coming, so I scooted myself over to the wall and stood up. After catching my breath and gently wiping the blood from my broken nose I quietly searched the room. It took me a long while to finally find a set of keys in the pocket of a huge coat draped over the desk chair I had no idea if they were the right ones or not, but they were all I could find. In a closet I also found Li's sword and Jacobs's gun belt. I found a bag of rifle shot and powder charges in a desk drawer. Li's bow was not around. I gathered everything up and peeked out the window. The guard was right there almost looking right at me. I ducked back in, heart pounding, and put my back against the wall. How was I going to get out of here? I had no idea what was through the door.

The door. With the rifle hanging above it. I had almost forgotten it!

I set the other things down and tip-toed toward the door. I couldn't reach the rifle, so I dragged the chair over, making more noise than I wanted. The rifle was an old single shot flintlock. An antique. I had no idea why Wasco would want it so badly. The stock was carved with an animal that looked like something from one of Ying's books. Like a lion but with three different heads. One was the lions, one a goat and the last looked like a dragon head. I climbed up and reached for it, but the damn thing was on hooks and even with the chair I couldn't get it over the hooks because I was too short!

I stretched up on my tip-toes trying to push it off the brass hooks, when all of a sudden, I knew something was wrong. I didn't know what it was or how I knew, but something screamed in my head to move, and move now!

I yanked as hard as I could. My feet came off the chair and it fell with a heavy thud. One of the hooks pulled free from the wall which spun me to the side and slammed my back into the wall. I slid down onto my ass, rifle in hand, as a spiked tail as thick as my torso plunged into the door where I had just been with a loud *kthunk*. I raised the gun. It was too long for me to hold steady and I knew it couldn't be loaded, but my body just did it. What else was it going to do? I squeezed the trigger and closed my eyes.

It roared in my ears and kicked against the wall. I opened my eyes slowly and peeked through the smoke. The scorpion-man was five feet away, tail still stuck fast in the door, stretched taut over its head. Greenish-black ichor ran from it down the door making a sickening puddle on the floor. It tilted his head and looked at me. Then its all-too-human eyes rolled up and crossed, like it was trying to see the dime-size hole the bullet had made in the center of its forehead, then it crumpled face-first to the floor. The hole in the back of its head was not as small and not as neat. I left what I had eaten that day on the floor next to it and sat there gasping until I heard boots on wood planks outside the door.

The body moved suddenly, and I leapt to my feet and backed away. Someone pulled on the door once more and the tail stretched tight and moved the body again. I could hear commotion starting around the camp. I slung the rifle over my shoulder by its strap as I ran across the room, picked up the gear, and climbed out the window. Once out I looked around. Nothing was looking my way, but I saw shadows moving across the light that was cast from inside. I ran as fast as I could for the cages, Jacob's gun belt bouncing along behind me. I got to the door without any of the monsters seeing me. They must have all been inside. When I reached the cage, everyone was on their feet, even Wasco. He looked very pale and was leaning heavily on Jacob.

I dropped everything to unlock the cage, but Wasco said, "Hand me Bella, girl."

He held his hand out through the bars. It was trembling.

I picked the long gun up and handed it to him, then handed the ammo and powder to Jacob. Then I went to the door with the keys.

Jacob mirrored me to the door and I started trying keys.

"Topher what's all that blood from?" he said.

"Oh, I..."

I looked down and saw I was covered in blood from my nose, but then it dawned on me that my broken nose no longer hurt, nor was it bleeding. I reached up to feel it. It was straight. Felt perfectly fine as a matter of fact.

"I, um, I busted my nose I guess. I'm fine, now shut up. I'm tryin' to do this!" I said.

Eventually I found the right key and the others grabbed their belongings. By now the camp was in full uproar and I could see brighter fires flaring up through the cracks in the door.

"How are we gonna get out of here? Wasco can barely walk!" I screamed.

I was starting to panic again and would have thrown up if I had anything left in me.

I looked over to Wasco. He was standing on his own. Not quite the rock of a man I was used to, but his breathing was normal, and he stood up straight without help. He still looked weaker than I had ever seen him, but more like a rock with a crack than the crumbled stone I had seen just a few minutes ago.

"What in Sam Hill is that thing?" I said looking at the rifle he was loading.

"You shot her didn't ya? Shouldn't have. Ain't time yet," he said.

"Wha? Listen you stupid yak, if it weren't fer me you wouldn't have that damn gun; and if I hadn't shot her — HER? What the hell, her? — if I hadn't had shot that damned gun, I'd be dead! So, shut up!" I screamed.

He looked up at me and squinted.

"Yeah, reckon so," he said. "You done good, girl. Now let's git out of here."

The door at the end of the hall kicked in and Wasco had Bella up to his shoulder and shot before they had taken a step. The ball took a man, just a regular looking man, dead in the chest and blasted him backward. Two men, at least their top halves were, tried to aim rifles inside but Jacob shot them first. The door slammed shut again. I, of course, had not brought the Winchester because I'm a chucklehead, so I didn't have a damn gun.

"Not getting out that way. I will go check down the hall," Jacob said and ran deeper into the building. The guy Wasco had shot had dropped his pistol in the door. Li ran over and picked it up, then handed it to me.

"I can't shoot this damn thing!" I said.

"It is better than having nothing, Topher," he said.

A call came in from outside. "Hey, y'all in there. We got enough men out here to storm ya. Why don't you just give up so nobody else gets shot? Ain't nowhere for ya to go. No other way out!"

"Anyone see how many men they got?" Wasco asked.

"From the tents and those I saw, I would guess there are about thirty men here," Li said.

"And a girl," I said. "Saw her room."

Wasco said, "When I scouted earlier the air ship was flying away. Maybe a bunch of them are on it. How long has it been?"

Jacob came trotting up the hall. "Been about three or four hours since we got here I'd guess," he said. "I might have found a way out, but you will not like it," Jacob said.

Wasco said, "Like it better than standin' here gettin' my ass shot off. Lead the way."

"There's more, Wasco." He pulled him closer to talk quieter. "There is some grisly sights up there I am not sure Topher needs to see."

Normally I would have chimed in to let him know where he could put that talk, but after everything I had seen, I wasn't sure I wanted to see it either.

"Ain't like we got a choice Jacob," Wasco said. "She's here, she's in it thick. Ain't no sense tryin' to baby her now. Let's go."

Li took the keys from the door of the cage and opened the one across from it. They almost hit each other. He ran in and unlocked a pair of manacles and locked the open gates to each other, and then we ran down the hallway.

CHAPTER TEN – BULL MCCAIN

The sight I ran into will never leave me. A horse was hanging in a sling some ten feet in the air. To say it was dead doesn't do justice to being dead. On a balcony to the side were large wooden tanks. Pipes ran out of them to some kind of machinery that had small tubes coming from it and going into the horse.

The horse was exsanguinated. Its eyes were completely black, open wide in fear and panic. But that's not the worst of it. Tubes also came out of the horse and down to more machinery, then a cage. The cage, though empty, was clearly designed for a person to be chained in. The tubes dangled nearby ending in long, stained needles. There were also tables with straps, stained with red and black, with tools hanging neatly on the wall that I cannot bear to even describe. There was a large barrel with a lid that had the same dark stains down the sides. In the corner was a desk that was disturbingly neat and tidy, as was the floor around it. It stood in such contrast to the horror around it that it might have been the most sickening sight of all. Not a paper was out of place. I heaved and heaved, but there was nothing left but bile.

"Look up there." Jacob pointed. "That sling is on a pivot, looks like to swing the bodies out the wall over there. If you get close you can see the door that opens. I saw the pile of bodies when we came in."

Wasco looked up then traced his gaze to the floor.

"That'll be more than a twenty-foot drop onto a lot of sharp bones. I ain't sure we'd all make it," he said.

A door being kicked in followed by gunfire interrupted the discussion and snapped me out of my breakdown. I ran over and peeked around the corner. They were standing by the cage doors Li had jammed. Some were human, some were something else. One small man with a disturbingly rat-like appearance worked his way to the front of the crowd, looked at the doors, then started squeezing through the space. Literally.

I could see his rib cage compress unnaturally, his shoulders twisted in a way no person should be able to move, but he did it without apparent discomfort and slid right through. When he turned and saw me he grinned and pulled out a long straight-bladed knife. I shot him in the crotch. I tried to shoot him in the chest, but I couldn't shoot the damn pistols, so I shot him in the crotch. It was messy, but I was numb to it all by then. He slumped back against the bars whimpering, which knocked into the guns that tried to fire my way and I jumped back. I had dropped the damn gun from the kick, but I wasn't about to stick my head around to get it.

"Topher! You okay?" Jacob called.

"Shot him in the balls," I said. "But they're gettin' a hacksaw I heard one of them say."

Jacob just stared at me.

"What, I didn't mean to! I told you I couldn't shoot a goddamned pistol!" I said.

He didn't say anything, just turned back to Wasco shaking his head.

"It's all we got Wasco, we either go out that door or we go against them things head on," he said.

"Maybe we can climb from the opening to the roof?" Li offered.

"Rather do that," Wasco said. "Let's check it out. Ain't gonna take them fellas long to get through that gate. Jacob, wanna send some lead their way so they think we're makin' a stand? Only way up is them boards, I don't know if I trust them to hold any of us adults."

He looked at me.

"Topher, can you get up there and hang a rope, make it easier for us old broke-downs?" he asked.

I looked up and nodded. My brain tried to find something smart-ass to say, but I was too tired.

"Ok, git up there and crack that door a bit and make sure they ain't watchin' it. If it's clear, see if there's something up there to tie this rope to. Gonna kill the lights in here once you're past the hard climb so they don't see the door opening."

Jacob started shooting while I climbed. I was never afraid of heights and loved to climb so that part was easy, but soon I was eye level with that horse. It was all I could do to keep from heaving my guts out again. Then Wasco thankfully put out all the lights. It took some looking to find the mechanism to open the door, and then I pushed it just a tiny bit and peeked out. There were five men down there.

Well sort of men, some of them were that mix of animal and man. They were looking into the door below. I guessed that some of them were supposed to be watching up here by their posture but got distracted by the bullets Jacob was sending at them. I looked up and saw the ledge of the roof within easy reach, pushed the door open a bit more, and saw the pile of bodies below me.

The sky spun around. I started heaving again, trying to be quiet but I couldn't do it. This was crazy. I was a damn kid. What the hell was I doing? I was going to end up in that pile, or worse, one of those things! I had to get out of here. Jump. Maybe I could jump over the pile and run. I had to run. If I didn't, I was going to fall into that pile and just die.

A light off in the distance stopped the spinning and the thinking. What was that? A small fire maybe, but it was growing. Not huge, but big enough for me to make out a shape. The shape of a dragon. A dragon made of fire that spread its tail out and waved it, like the one I had seen with Ying.

Ying was out there!

It took to the air and started to fly straight toward me. When it got close to the camp it veered away and plunged into one of the tents, setting it ablaze, then poured out into another and was gone. But it left two tents burning and that sent many of the men scrambling for water. I grabbed the ledge and pulled myself over and onto the roof, then started looking for somewhere to tie the rope off. As I turned I saw a dark shape in the sky. Like a big square. Like a sail. Sonofabitch! The sky ship! I tied the rope off to the chimney, tossed the other end back through the window, and then followed it in.

"That ship is coming back, hurry up!" I called.

The rope snapped taut and Wasco came up. I heard Jacob exclaim in pain, then more guns.

"Go, I'll hold them." Jacob's voice sounded strained.

. Li was up next and moved to Wasco who was moving to go back down.

"We must get away from the edge of the roof. Now. He is hurt. She need not see what is to come," Li said.

They stared at each other for a long time.

Wasco nodded.

"Reckon so. Let's go Topher. Jacob's got work to do then he'll be along."

He spit over the side, before turning. I stood there a minute trying to decide what to do. We couldn't leave Jacob! I turned to yell that at Wasco and met his eyes. They were like rocks pinning me in place.

"Ya swore to me girl," he said. "Now let's go. Ya need to trust me. To trust him."

I went. Damnit I went. We ran across the roof for a ways, and then Wasco stopped, brought his rifle up to his shoulder, and started aiming for the ship. After a second or two he squeezed the trigger. I don't know what he hit, but the ship dipped sharply to the right and I saw the silhouettes of men falling from the side. Damn he was good. We ran across the roof to the other end of the building. Wasco reloading and firing on the run at men on the ground. Another fiery dragon came shooting in and set more tents on fire. When we reached the edge, we scooted down to lowest part and Wasco shimmied off. He hung by his fingertips then dropped. Li was next, then me. I was too scared to be scared. Wasco and Li made sure I landed okay; the fall wasn't that far on this side.

We were getting back to our feet and ready when a man with the head of a desert lion came around the corner. In the blink of an eye he leapt at me, clawed hands reaching out. Li cut it down with one swipe of his sword, blood making an arc in the sand. Wasco bent and took the pistol from his belt and gave it to me with a shrug.

I scowled and said, "I can't shoot these things!"

"Let's go," he said.

We rounded the corner and came to another door. Li stopped.

"The fire rifle is inside, I must retrieve it," he said.

He kicked out at the door and it swung off its hinges, and then he ran into the building and down the hall. We followed. The first room was an open area that looked like sleeping quarters for animals and men. Or men that are part animal. There were stalls with hay on the floor, beds, and a pit with sand covering the floor.

We ran on, Li leading the way. Everyone must have been outside fighting fires because we didn't encounter anyone. A roar shattered the night and set the hairs on my neck on end. Then gunfire erupted in earnest at the other end of the building where Jacob was.

"What was that?" I said.

"Don't matter girl, we got to move," Wasco said and gave me a gentle shove after Li, who had disappeared into another room.

He came out holding the rifle. "No ammo, but at least I have recovered it."

"I have some. Found it on Wasco's horse."

"Good girl. Li, give her that thing, she can shoot it." He handed me some powder loads.

Li hesitated until Wasco turned to face him. He handed me the rifle and I loaded it.

Wasco said, "Save at least one of them fire rounds Topher; need to make sure we burn this madhouse to the ground before we leave. Now, we got no choice. That ship might have a lot of monsters and men on it. We got to get clear of here before that ship lands. You up fer this, kid?"

"Yeah, I can shoot monsters, and I ain't sure the men that made 'em ain't the worst of them," I said, sounding braver than I was.

"Good girl. Li?"

Li was tucking the pistol I had been carrying into his wide cloth belt. He looked up and nodded.

"All right then. We keep shooting until we run out of ammo. Grab guns as you go. Topher, you get down to that last round, you shoot it into this building."

I nodded my head.

"Li, I ain't gonna tell you how to do what it is you do, but if you can keep 'em off me while I reload, I'd be much obliged"

Li nodded. "I will do what I can."

"Make for the front gate; if we get separated we meet back where the camp was. Topher, best you stay near me."

Out the door and into hell we went. There were flames everywhere; I thought I saw little figures dancing in them, fanning them larger. Around the corner from the pile of bodies was a ruckus that had men running toward it and then away. A giant snake with a man's head came flying over the building and landed in a heap. Wasco brought the rifle up and fired and a half-man half-horse fell. Then Li was out amongst them cutting men and monsters down. Most were too busy with whatever was around that corner to know we were there at first. By the time they figured it out it was too late for most of them. I only fired one shot. I don't even know if I hit the thing I was aiming at. The path to the gate was clear, most of the fighting was over, and what was left was around the corner. I turned to ask Wasco if I should shoot the building, then he was gone.

It happened so fast I didn't register what had transpired at first. One second, he was there, the next he was just gone. Then my brain caught up to my eyes and I saw it. Where Wasco had been stood a hulking mass of meat and muscle. A man with a bull's head stood bent over from the charge that had landed Wasco fifteen feet away. It wore fine looking trousers and boots with a button up shirt that had little triangle-shaped buttons that looked familiar. I remember thinking he should have a ring in his nose. Bulls always had rings in their noses. It looked at me, and snorted dismissively, and then it looked to Li.

It said, "Well, do you want to give up, or do you want me to kill you?

It didn't sound anything like it looked. It sounded cultured, like an Englishman.

Li's sword snapped up almost in a salute, and then he fell into a fighting stance, sword held straight out, eyeing the monster cautiously.

Me? I shot the son of a bitch.

Fire blasted across the thing's broad chest and engulfed its face. I didn't wait to see what happened next. I was already reloading. Li jumped at it, sword swinging in to disembowel it. It connected but only left a small line of blood, the tough hide and muscle turning most of the blade away.

Li reversed his momentum and came back in with a series of stabs and slashes that opened little lines of blood all over its arms that had been raised in a protective posture. It looked to be on its heels until one of its muscled arms shot out with frightening speed and snatched Li's sword hand in a huge leathery hand, crushing Li's hand around the sword's grip. I heard the bones crunch and Li was lifted from the ground and into the flames still licking up the monster's chest.

The bull brought him face to face and said, "Little man. I gave you a choice. You chose wrong."

The massive arm snapped, and Li flew the length of the courtyard before slamming into the side of the building with a sickening crunch. I was reloading as fast as I could, but I was no Wasco. It took two steps and the same hand snapped out and knocked the rifle from my hands. The rifle clipped me in the chin as it flew, and I reeled. The Bull, who I guessed was Bull McCain, ripped the flaming shirt he was wearing off and threw it at me. I rolled away.

"I don't like hurting kids. But you shot me. You burned me. You burned my shirt. And it hurt. So, I am going to make an exception and stomp your scrawny ass into the ground," it said, and its giant hoof of a foot scraped the black sand.

"Reckon that would be a mistake," Wasco said walking towards the Bull with purpose, Bella already at his shoulder.

The gun roared and so did the Bull. Where the fire annoyed him, Bella made him bleed. The bullet hit him in the chest with a burst of blood and bone chips, but I heard it go whizzing off into the night. The wound bled, but it wasn't critical. Wasco was already reloading when the Bull charged him. Wasco proved faster, stepped around to the side, and got another shot off. This one caught the flesh on Bull's massive bicep and left a hole clean through. It roared and spun faster than seemed possible.

I finished reloading the rifle I hadn't even known I'd picked up and was watching for an opening when I saw horses come around the corner. Or what I thought were horses at first. They had horse bodies, but instead of horse heads they had men's upper torsos. They stood in two perfect lines and wore uniforms I didn't recognize. Each carried a new-looking steam rifle tipped with a blade, which they lowered at me and Wasco. I knew I was dead. Wasco looked at me and I read sadness in his eyes. That scared me more than anything ever had.

Then something crashed into their line. It was giant, massively muscled while being oddly emaciated, and antlers grew out of an almost human-looking head. It dove into them with hungry abandon. The force of its charge knocked one off its feet and it tore into its horse flesh with gnashing teeth and clawed hands before leaping onto the back of the next one. There was chaos and blood and gore in seconds. It lifted one of the horsemen over its head, ripped a chunk from its belly with impossibly long teeth and tossed it into the rest, then followed it in, entrails trailing from the body and the monster's jaws. I watched, unable to look away as a creature that had to be from Hell bit, chewed, and swallowed huge bites from anything it could get its hands on.

I wanted to throw up again, but my body didn't have the energy or the substance. I wanted to run, but I couldn't take my eyes off that strange creature that had saved us in the most gruesome way. I just stood watching, until something knocked all the air from my lungs. I was thankfully thrown to the ground, the rifle again flying from my grasp. The Bull had barely clipped me, its heavy-hoofed foot barely missing my head in its pursuit of Wasco, who was still moving, reloading, and firing with a rhythm and speed that defied the man's size.

Wasco's rifle sounded off again and more blood flew from the beast, though it seemed not to notice. I saw at least four bleeding holes in Bull left by Bella, but he hadn't slowed in the least and was within feet of Wasco now.

I ran to the rifle and dug for the last fire ball, reloaded, and leveled the barrel at the Bull's back, tracking him as he gave chase. My focus expanded as he crossed in front of the building where Li had hit. The boards had shattered, and I could see Li's body lying limp in the debris. I needed to burn that building down, not shoot at a monster that wouldn't even notice. To do that, I needed to get Li out of there.

I pulled the rifle from my shoulder, ran to the building and climbed through, the broken lumber ripping my hand open in the process. Li was lying just inside, one of his arms hung ruined on a nail that had torn through the flesh. It looked like he was waving, except his arm was at an angle that was impossible. I didn't know how to help him, I knew nothing about doctoring.

"Li," I said, touching his face. "Li, what do I do? Your arm, it's broke. I gotta get you out of here!"

"No child. You do not. I am not leaving here. Please take my sword to Mistress Ying. Then do what you must. This place is an abomination to the spirits and must be destroyed."

His voice was soft, but strong. Stronger than seemed possible given his broken body.

"Bullcrap Li!" I screamed. "I can't just leave you here! You'll die!"

"No child," he said. "I am already dead."

With that proclamation I saw what my mind had refused to see before. His mouth had not been moving. He had not been breathing. I looked up from the body and to the faint glowing mist as it collapsed from vaguely human looking into a formless cloud and trailed gently toward the sword that lay a few feet away. It swirled around it as if being pulled in.

The room was blurry through my tears. I don't know how long I cried there alone in that dirty perverted building, but when I came to my senses I knew I had to burn it down. It was, as Li had said, an abomination. Bull was an abomination. He had killed Li without even a thought. I looked out the hole in the wall and saw Wasco take a full-on punch from Bull that sent teeth flying. He reeled but returned a punch that set the massive man-bull back a small step. Bull held a knife now and Wasco had his tomahawk in one hand, Bella in the other. I watched as Bull plunged the knife into Wasco's side. He must have hit something because the blood pumped out, as if in tune to a fast-beating heart. Wasco spun away, grunting as the knife slid out with another gout of blood. He followed his spin around and delivered a fierce backhanded chop to Bull's thigh with his axe. As he turned I was able to see the wound clearly, or what should have been a wound at least. There was blood, but no longer the spray of a severed artery. Now there was a faint trickle from a wound that could not seriously be called a scratch!

I stumbled back in awe, both of the incredible things I had just witnessed and the sheer force of the two combatants. My foot kicked the sword lying by Li's dead hand. It startled me awake and I bent and picked it up. It felt warm. I felt my body relax a little and my breathing slowed. I removed his scabbard, which was not easy, and slung the sword over my back. Its tip was hitting me in the calf when I ran, but I was able to manage. I ran through the building knocking over oil lamps and throwing anything flammable I could into the long center hall. When I reached the last room, I turned and shot the last of the fire bullets into the pile. It went up with a whoosh that pulled the air from my lungs and drove me out the window.

I rolled, in a not very graceful tumble, and got to my feet, still clinging to the empty fire rifle. All was quiet. The fighting seemed to be over. I didn't hear or see anyone on this side of the building. But for the smoking husks of tents and bodies you'd never know there had just been a horrific battle. I ran back toward the place Wasco and Bull had been fighting. I came around the corner to see Wasco lying in a fresh water tank. Not the blackish crap from the mines but one full of fresh water that was clear, except for the spreading pool of dark blood coming from Wasco. He was still, one arm floating limp in the water, the other holding Bella, his nose and mouth barely above the water. Bull was reaching to take Bella from his hand. He didn't look much better than Wasco, except that he was still standing.

He turned to look at me as I skidded to a stop.

"I'll be damned," he said. "You are one tough little kid. I can't believe you're still alive. I think I'll find something just as tough to mix you with. A wolverine maybe? Small, fierce. Yeah, I think that'll work. I'll make you a furry little attack dog," he sneered.

The expression just didn't carry on his animalistic Bull face. Looked more like he had something stuck in his teeth.

I pointed at the burning building.

"You ain't doin' shit, pig-face; I burned your stupid animal circus down!" I said.

I'd like to think I was being brave, but I was just mad. I guess he hadn't noticed the fire because he looked surprised when he looked over and saw the flames reaching up from the building. Just then the roof collapsed in a cloud of flame and ash.

He said, "Aw kid. Why'd you go and do that? Well, no matter, you're a girl, anyway, aren't you? Didn't notice at first. I don't think her magic would work on you anyway. Guess I'll just have to kill you. Give me one second, I want this rifle, it fits me."

He pointed at Bella's stock. "That carving right there, it's called a chimera. It's a monster that is a mix of different animals." He winked at me. "Seems right that I ought to have it don't you think?"

He grabbed Bella and pulled. Wasco's arm moved, but his hand didn't let go. He pulled again, harder. Nothing. He glanced back at me. I stuck my tongue out at him and flipped him off. He turned back and growled and yanked. Wasco's body jerked, lifted, but his hand did not release Bella. Bull let it go and Wasco slid down under the water, only his arm sticking out, still holding the rifle like he was offering it to the sky.

Bull turned back to me. "I'm going to need that pigsticker you've got there so I can cut his hand off."

Then he started walking towards me.

I had three things. A sword I couldn't begin to use, an empty rifle, and my spitshot I always kept loaded in my pocket.

His walk became a trot, and then he charged at me. Although he was much slower than he had been before and with a definitive limp, he was still coming fast.

I grabbed the spitshot, hocked up the biggest spit I could and let fire. I didn't try and run, there was no use and I was too mad. Besides, I needed to aim. I hit him right in the nose. My pa had told me once he could lead around the biggest bulls in the Empire by rings in their noses, because that part of the nose was sensitive. Turns out he was right.

Bull pulled up and stopped as the Blackchip, followed by a trail of steam, hit him just inside of his flaring nostril. He even turned with the impact as if he had been steered for just a step or two. It was all I needed. I ran by him, sliding by his massive legs, stood, and made for the water tank. I grabbed for Bella, hoping to pull Wasco's head out of the water by it and wake him up. I could hear Bull stomping up behind me.

The rifle slid easily from Wasco's grasp and I tumbled backwards into the water, gulped half the water from the tank, and stood up coughing. I knew he was right behind me so like before I just did what my body said I should. I turned and squeezed the trigger. This time managing to keep my eyes open, but barely able to hold the long gun up, let alone steady. Bull was reaching for me when the bullet hit him in the chest. He stumbled back, caught himself, and still came on.

I fell backwards with the kick of the gun and tumbled over and onto Wasco, dropping Bella. I reached into my vest and pulled out the little vial Ying had given me just as Bull crashed through the side of the water tank. Wood and water flew in every direction and Wasco's head surfaced. I shoved the whole vial into Wasco's mouth and scrabbled across the tank. Bull stomped over Wasco and reached for me. I backpedaled as fast as I could. He came on, having been slowed only slightly by the tank and water. My back hit the wall of the tank, there was nowhere left to go.

Bella snapped across Bull's massive neck and I saw Wasco pull himself up by the rifle. He then braced his knees against Bull's back and pulled. Bull fell to a knee, and reached up trying to grab at Wasco, snorting and grunting, then fell face-first into the almost-empty tank. One of his horns ripped into my leg on its way down and blood poured out. Wasco clung to Bella, the muscles in his arms standing out like boulders as he pulled the rifle against the wounded Bull's throat. The thrashing lasted a few very long minutes and then Bull was still. Wasco fell from the massive back and hit the wooden floor of the tank with a dull thud. I was pinned against the far side of the now-drained tank, the weight of the monster holding me fast and having the horn shoved clean through my leg. I was losing blood fast. Blackness started to creep in on me. I was getting real tired of that feeling.

CHAPTER ELEVEN – WENDIGO

I woke up to a cold dark night sky. I could smell smoke heavy in the air and there was a glow off to my right.

The fort.

I turned my head and found Wasco sitting against a rock, maybe a Mover, staring out into the night. Ying was curled up on her side by the fire. There was no sign of Jacob or Li. The memory of Li's body came flooding back to me and I sobbed. Wasco's head snapped over to me.

"Ya alright girl?" he asked.

His voice was quiet, soft.

"Li's dead," I said. "I tried to help him, but I couldn't and he's dead."

"I know. Weren't nothin' ya coulda done. He was dead afore you got to him," he said.

I remembered the sword and started groping for it. It was lying on the ground next to me and I picked it up.

"He told me to give this to, Ying," I said.

"It can wait till mornin', git some sleep."

"I can't sleep no more," I said and sat up.

Ying sat up as well and looked at me. "There was nothing you could do to save him Christopher. I knew of his passing when it happened. He is at peace and has rejoined his ancestors."

I couldn't speak. I just sobbed. I stood up and walked to her, holding the sword out.

"He said I needed to bring this to you."

"So he did, and so you have."

She took it from my shaking hand. And another sob escaped from my treacherous mouth. I'd had about enough of it always letting out sounds I didn't want others hearing.

"Sit," she said.

I did, and she took my hands in her small wrinkled hands. They were soft. She looked at me. "Christopher, Li has passed on, but he is not gone. This sword is the Sword of Ancestors. It has been in his family for a very long time. Generations. All wielded this weapon for one purpose, and to die in the performance of that duty is an honor. To Li, and to those who held the sword before him, there is no greater honor than to die doing what they dedicated their lives to with this sword, and they live on within it."

I just stared at her. I mean, yes, I had seen walking rocks, and half-animal men, and God knows what else, but my young mind just couldn't wrap around whatever she was trying to say. He lived in the sword? What did that even mean?

She smiled, patted my hand, and picked up Li's sword.

"Do you see these marks?" she asked.

She pointed to a series of marks along the blade. It looked like the Chinese writing I had seen on many of the things in her shop.

"Yes, what does it say?" I asked.

"They are names," she said. "The names of every person that has carried this sword and died while performing their duty."

"Is, is Li's name on it?" I asked.

"It is not child, not yet," she said.

She pulled the sword from the sheath. It seemed to glow in the night. She laid it across her lap, reached out and took my hand and placed it on the hilt. My hand was shaking so hard the sword shook on Ying's knees and almost fell off.

Ying put her hand over mine until the shaking stopped.

"The responsibility for bringing the spirit of Li forth falls to the one he gave his life in service to. That was me, young Christopher. His family pledged to protect those of my line and to give their lives if necessary. If they performed their duties with honor and they died in the effort, it then falls to the Elder to insure his spirit is brought forth into the sword. I wish for you to help me with this ceremony, Christopher. Li would wish it as well."

I could not do anything more than nod. I didn't really understand what she was talking about, but the tone of her voice and the way that she looked at me left no question I was going to do as she asked.

We didn't say anything for a long time when it was done. We just sat and watched the stars turn.

I was holding the sword on my chest, looking up into the night when a thought hit me.

"Ying," I said in a quiet voice. "You said that the Guardian's name would be put on the sword and his spirit held there if he died with honor."

"That is correct, Christopher."

"What would have happened if he didn't?"

She was quiet for many breaths before answering. She inhaled and said, "Had I not performed the ceremony, his spirit would have been cast from the sword."

"Would he have gone to Heaven then? Hell? Would we have sent Li to Hell if he didn't do everything he was supposed to!"

I could hear the smile in her response.

"No child, he would not have gone to Heaven or to Hell, at least as you know them. There are more places for spirits in the universe than those, Christopher. But those are lessons for another day. As to Li, I cannot imagine I would have done anything other than the Honoring, regardless of the circumstances. As I said, it is the choice of the Elder."

I pondered that for a long time. I swear I could feel Li's steady personality through the sword. I eventually dozed off.

When I woke up it was still deep night. Wasco still sat his vigil looking out into the desert. I didn't know what he was looking for or at, but he definitely seemed pensive. I kept sneaking looks at him out of the corner of my eye. He turned his head and caught me once, then just went back to looking out into the darkness for,

"*Jacob*!" I cried jumping to my feet and regretting it immediately. I stumbled as my leg gave out and I went to my knees. "What happened to Jacob? He didn't die, did he? He couldn't have! How could you leave him? We have to go back!"

I could not believe I had been there all that time and had not thought about Jacob. What kind of monster was I?

Wasco didn't move. "We tried kid. We tried. I couldn't find no sign of him. Not dead. Not alive."

"That is why we are still here child. I believe he is close. If he is, he will find us," Ying said from her bedroll.

I sobbed myself to sleep with my arms around Ying and woke up in the morning with a hole in my heart that hurt more than all my wounds. I saw Wasco packing up the camp but had no energy to complain. I knew he wouldn't leave if he thought there was any chance. I laid there until Ying said it was time to go. Once everything was ready we climbed into our saddles and started out of the nightmare that was the Blacklands.

I noticed as we headed out, that one horse was still loosely hobbled in the circle, munching on some grass. Black with a white diamond on its head. A saddle and pack was stuck between two rocks.

The ride back was blessedly uneventful and, since we knew where we were going, much quicker than the trip in. It seemed like no time at all had passed and we were out of the Blacklands.

I woke up under the cold starry night sky wondering where I was at first, then why I was awake. We were just a couple of days outside of Edge City and nothing had threatened us. I could even see the city lights from the hill we were on. I saw Wasco sleeping to my left, and Ying, again curled as close to the fire as she could get. I knew Wasco slept very lightly and figured had there been any danger, he would have been awake. I tried to close my eyes but couldn't. I felt something. I started to shiver.

"Wasco," I called softly. He didn't stir. I tried again a little louder, starting to panic.

"What is it kid?" he answered in a quiet growl, but I saw his hand in the darkness fall slowly to Bella.

"I think somethin's out there. I dunno why, I just feel it," I said.

"Might be yer right," he said. "Ying?"

"I am awake Mr. Wasco," came her soft answer.

"Can you light up that fire a bit real fast?" Wasco asked. "Like you done before?"

"I can. Both of you look right at it for a moment. Get your eyes used to the light. Look to a bright spot. Ok, on my command close your eyes and look away, now!" she said.

I could see the light from behind my closed lids as the fire shot upward. I heard Wasco jump to his feet and I scrambled to mine. Out maybe twenty feet was a horse with a man draped over it. A black horse with a white diamond on its forehead.

"*Jacob*!" I yelled and ran over to him in a hopping limp. He was glassy-eyed and not coherent. Wasco showed up and pulled him off the horse. He carried Jacob into the now-diminished firelight and I led the horse over and tied him with the others. Jacob was laid out on a bedroll by the time I limped back, cursing myself for having tried to run. I felt new blood running down my leg from the wound but paid it no mind.

Jacob was naked as a jaybird; Ying covered his privates with a sheet and looked him over for wounds. He didn't look injured, but he was covered in blood. Ying confirmed he was physically okay.

"I'm okay," he groaned. "Just had a hard time getting out of there alone. Was hard not to..." He looked over at me. "Was hard is all."

"Git some rest," Wasco said. "You can tell us yer story in the morning." Wasco patted him on the shoulder and stood up. "I'm glad ya made it, Snake."

I didn't sleep much the rest of the night, but I managed some. In the morning I realized that my leg had bled quite a bit and I swooned. Ying scolded me and rewrapped it with some of her stinky salve. Wasco called me a dunce, then we sat around the fire eating some hard bread and drinking coffee and tea.

It was odd watching Ying fix her own tea and it made me sad again. Li had usually made it before Ying got up. She seemed sad as well, but said nothing about it, just went about the tasks of the morning methodically.

After a bit I noticed Wasco and Jacob looking at each other for a long while.

"I think it's time ya told yer tale, Jacob," Wasco said. "Can't keep goin' like this forever. I'm guessin' Ying there knows a bit of it and I got some guesses, but it needs to come from your mouth. I know ya think yer doin' right by her, keeping it in, but ya ain't. So, spill it."

Jacob took a sip of the hot coffee and glanced my way. For my part I had no idea what they were talking about.

"What?" I said.

"Wasn't because I thought I was doing right by her." He looked back to Wasco. "It was because I am a coward and I didn't want her to be afraid of me," Jacob said.

"I ain't afraid of you, chucklehead!"

"I know," he said grinning, "was hoping to keep it that way. I am cursed. By Natives. Cree Nation." He looked at Wasco who nodded.

"So?" I said. "We'll go make 'em take it off ya. Wasco can talk to them."

Jacob said. "I...um. Well that is. Let me start from the beginning and maybe that will help me get to it. I'm a gun for hire. Always have been. From the first time my father put a pistol in my hand I wanted to be a gunfighter. Wanted to be famous. Ran with a couple of less-than-upright gangs for a bit, but it never really sat well with me. So, I went out on my own for hire. Made a pretty good reputation for myself without crossing too many lines I didn't want to cross.

"Then I hired on with the Cooper Railway. The job was simple. Ride trail in front of the workers, make sure there were no disruptions. It was easy money, right up until we crossed near, or into, the Cree Nation. Boss said we were on the right side, the Cree, they disagreed strongly. It was an ugly couple of weeks, and I killed more men than I should have for that damn railroad.

"One day, long after we had crossed the area in question we were ambushed by Cree warriors and I was taken to answer for my crimes."

He took a deep breath, and then continued. "I was never what I consider an evil man. I killed men yes, and for money. But I never killed a man that didn't have a chance to fight back and I let just as many live. It may seem a small thing, but it wasn't to me or to the Cree people. I was given a chance to redeem myself. Others on my team were not. I do not know which of us were the lucky ones."

He looked at me, then away and sipped his coffee. I was so caught up in the story that the details hadn't really sunk in. He took another deep breath and looked to Wasco. Wasco's face told nothing, he just nodded.

Jacob said, "I was cursed by the shaman council to, well, to make things right. To defend any of Native blood. Until such a time as my spirit is cleansed of the deeds I have done, I would carry the spirit of the Wendigo."

He let the word hang in the air, looking down at the ground. Nobody said anything for a long while.

Wasco growled, "Yeah, I figured it was a thing like that."

"What the hell is a Wendigo?" I said. I had no idea what they were talking about.

Ying answered. "It is a spirit of hunger and greed that can never be satiated. Is that correct Jacob?"

"That's the gist of it, Ying, yes. But it is worse than that. It is a monster that lurks inside of me. That craves the flesh of evil men. I am able to contain it most of the time. But when I become injured it can get free. I am healed of injury when it takes me, but its actions are..." He looked at me again, "horrible. It eats people Topher. I eat people." He began sobbing.

Ying placed her small hand on his, but he didn't seem to notice. I did. She was not afraid of him. Did not think him a monster. I looked at Wasco. His face was as unreadable as stone. He met my gaze then looked back to Jacob.

"Ain't a thing you can fix," Wasco said. "Or control. Least ways not right now. Reckon we all got our monsters. You get a chance to earn clear of yours. Can't blame a man fer that. So, you helpin' me and comin' along. I know that little bit I offered ya ain't what a gunman of your reputation should make. You took it 'cause you had to?"

Jacob said, "I did. The shaman elder said I needed to help those of Native blood and take the blood of evil men. When the Wendigo's thirst is sated, it will leave me. You said you had Native blood. Simple enough from there. Plus, you weren't too much of an ass."

"Girl, you got anything to say?" Wasco asked.

"I saw you," I said. "In the fight at the fort, I saw you. You saved me. I was scared, and it weren't pretty what you did, but you clearly went after the guys that were about to shoot us. I was just as close as they was. Easier target even. I figure it don't matter how you did it. You lived and yer here with us again. We'll just keep findin' ya Natives to help."

That was the end of it. He hugged me; I hugged him back, even though I wasn't much for all that hugging. Made me feel weird. But I hugged him, he cried, and we moved on.

Sitting at the small table at Ying's, Li's absence was more evident. He would normally be shuffling around the shop in his little slippers doing this and that while everyone talked, piping in here or there. Now he was gone. I looked up at the sword sitting in the corner and smiled. *No, not gone*, I thought.

Ying had sent a boy to find me and asked me to come see her. Ma had not been home since we got back a few days ago, and I had not heard from her. I was hoping Ying had heard something. She had.

"Christopher," she began, "I have news from the mines about your mother."

I knew what she was going to say before she said it. I didn't cry. I think I had already known. I think I knew before we left. Ying gave me the package from Keaton Industries. It had a nicely typed letter, a few coins that were her pay, and a payment for my pain and suffering. Her belongings were wrapped up in the bottom of the package. A few head scarves, a dress, some cheap jewelry, a small vial of stinky perfume, and a photo of me.

There wasn't anything else to do. There was no body to burn because she had died in a cave in. Nobody really knew who owned our tiny house, so it was just mine I supposed. Just like that I was an orphan. But I guess I really had been since Pa had left for the Empire. Ma always cared for me, but she was never the same. Now it had just become official.

I stayed with Ying for the next week while I let everything sink in and my leg heal some. By week's end I was limping down my cramped, smelly ally. The same way I had not so long ago when Wasco first came out of the mountains rolling up to the gate. The blanket that had been my door was gone. That was okay, I could get another. They probably needed it. Inside some snow had blown in, but nothing else was missing. The old canvas bag was still lying on the bed where I had left it. I went over and took the spyglass out of my belt and slipped it back into the bag. Then I pulled it back out and tucked it back into my belt. I started looking through the bag but just lost interest. It was bits of a family I didn't really know. A past that was so far away now it might have belonged to someone else. I climbed into the bed and slept.

I let the other orphans stay in the house whenever they wanted, and some nights I stayed at Ying's. She always asked me to stay for good, but I always said no and went back to my one-room shack. Time crept by with nothing happening to mark the amazing adventure that had swept me in its wake. Nothing marked the passing of my ma from this earth, the world just kept on as if nothing had changed. As if Wasco, Jacob, and I had not walked into the Blacklands and found it full of monsters. It was my first real understanding of how little the world cared about our wars and concerns, it just kept going.

I walked into Ying's shop a month or so later to the usual musical clinking of bamboo chimes. Wasco and Jacob greeted me. A warm smile and a hug from Jacob and what in Wasco terms was a face-splitting smile that to most people looked like the corner of his mouth twitched.

"How ya doin' kid?" Wasco asked.

"Better than you it smells like," I said and pinched my nose.

"Reckon so," he said. "Been on the trail. Came back as soon as we figured it all out."

"Figured what out?" I asked nodding at the papers strewn over the table.

"What do they say?"

"They say there was a lot of them animal-man things made in that place. Hundreds, maybe thousands," Wasco growled.

"Couldn't have been that many, camp weren't big enough," I said.

"Exactly Topher. So, the question is, where are they?" Jacob said.

"So, where are they? I asked. "They're pretty easy to spot ya know?"

Wasco said, "Yeah, unless they ain't nowhere to be spotted by anyone that would care. We told Keaton where to get his airship, but not till after we got a look in it ourselves."

"Wait. You went back there without me?"

Wasco said, "Yeah kid, we did. And we might again. It was spur-of-the-moment. 'Sides, I can't take you every time I go, can I?

I wasn't sure, but I didn't say anything.

"We went and told Keaton 'bout what we found, agreed to lead his boys to the ship," Wasco said.

"When we were close enough Wasco took off in the night to get a look at the ship before they did," Jacob said.

"Found these. Shipping manifests," Jacob said. They were not detailed, but they definitely show that the ship was selling something to people in the Empire. High-ranking people."

"Only them pompous asses use titles like *that*," Wasco added, pointing at a page.

"Best we can figure, is that they were making those things to sell to the Empire," Jacob said.

Wasco said, "I got a feelin' that Keaton knows somethin' more than he was lettin' on, too. I ain't convinced that Bull coulda stolen away an airship and Keaton would leave it be for so long. Somethin' smells like manure to me."

"That Bull McCain was dressed awful nice for a bandit in the wilds of the Blacklands, that's for sure. Silver buttons, shiny boots," Jacob said.

It hit me like a kick to the gut. I dug into my pocket and took out the little silver button I had found at Keaton's place. I looked at it, and then tossed it on the table.

"That's one of them fancy buttons Bull had on his shirt," I said.

They looked at me, but nobody said anything. They probably never got a chance to see them, what with me setting him on fire and all that.

"It's one of Bull's buttons, you chuckleheads! But I didn't get it off him; I got it from Keaton's place! It was on the floor in that lift thing!"

Ying looked up from her work. Wasco and Jacob both looked from me, then at each other, and back to me.

"Ya sure girl?" Wasco asked.

"Course I'm sure! I know where I steal stuff from!"
"Sonofabitch." Wasco said.
"Son of a bitch indeed," Jacob echoed.

Thank you for reading! If you like the book, please leave a review on Amazon and Goodreads. Even if you don't like it, please still leave a review.

Michael Conley is a veteran of the Desert Storm who has been telling stories in one form or another for his whole life. When the disabilities that came with his service threatened to limit his ability to do the outdoor work he enjoyed, he decided it was time to write some of the stories down.

He has his BA in Studio Art, with a focus on welded steel sculpture and pencil drawing, and now on the written word.

He's published short stories in the Urban Fantasy, Western Fantasy, Sci Fi and Fantasy genres.

He lives and writes on ten acres in Ohio with the woman of his dreams in the home of his dreams and as many dogs as he can manage.

You can follow Michael on Facebook at Michael Conley, author.